The Dragons of Summer

An Uncharted Realms Novella

by

Jeffe Kennedy

As unofficial consort to the High Queen, former mercenary Harlan Konyngrr faces a challenge worse than looming war and fearsome dragons. His long-held secrets threaten what he loves most—and he must make a choice between vows to two women.

Takes place after The Arrows of the Heart

Dedication

To everyone who loves Ursula and Harlan,
and asked for more.

Acknowledgements

Many thanks to my Fabulous Assistant Carien, who suggested several ideas that made this novella come to life—and who caught some egregious typos.

Thanks to Marcella Burnard and Jim Sorenson who provided very helpful feedback on the story and made it ever so much better.

So much love and appreciation to Rebecca Cremonese, for crying at all the right parts, and for being a sap in exactly the perfect way.

~ 1 ~

"**I**NSPECTING THE DEFENSES yet again?"

Ursula's question startled me, as I'd been so deep in thought I'd missed her approach. From my vantage on the walls of Castle Ordnung, I'd been contemplating the lush, green, and apparently peaceful countryside. The early onset of summer seemed to please the locals. For farmers and merchants, the fair weather brought welcome warmth for crops and dry roads for trade.

For a warrior like me, dry roads meant enemy forces could reach the seat of the Thirteen Kingdoms all that much more easily—and fair weather only made it easier to pillage freely and set fire to the rest.

I didn't let Ursula see she'd surprised me—or the dark direction of my thoughts. As High Queen of the Thirteen Kingdoms, she had enough to think about. "It pays to be thorough," I told her, making sure I looked relaxed.

"And here you're always nattering at me to delegate. Don't you have lieutenants to handle this?" she asked in an arch tone, her gaze as piercing as a hawk's. Sometimes her eyes are steely, like the sword she'd slept with when I met her, and other times they soften to gray with hints of blue, like the fog that rises out of the valleys of the Wild Lands in the mountains beyond Ordnung.

I've never told her that, as she'd be embarrassed—and would likely try to hide that softness from me. My Essla—as her sisters called her, a soft, intimate nickname I loved—learned long ago to compensate for her early wounds with tensile strength and hardening her heart.

Her tough resilience only added to Ursula's unique beauty. The rising sun set her deep auburn hair on fire, gilding her high cheekbones and that strong nose I'd set with my own hands after her father broke it. Dressed for court—though she had yet to don her crown—she wore a streamlined and high-necked gown of black velvet. A bodice of worked silver hugged her waist and flared over her elegant breasts, finishing with stylized caps at the shoulders. One of her mother's rubies glittered at the low dip in the center, where a pendant might rest on another woman.

Overall, the bodice gave the impression of armor, and Ursula's sheathed sword hung from the belt incorporated into the metalwork, the ruby in its hilt a perfect match to the one at her breast. The split skirt of the gown parted to reveal narrow silver leggings and high black leather boots beneath, allowing Ursula the freedom of movement she craved, even though she'd be waging battles of wits in the day ahead, not of arms.

We'd only returned a few weeks back, to fortify Ordnung and for Ursula to direct war strategy from the seat of the High Throne. To Ursula's vocal and caustic dismay, she had also returned to a veritably endless supply of gowns appropriate for court. The dressmaker, Denise, and her army of seamstresses had been hard at work during our journeys, creating formal garb so well designed for Ursula that she couldn't find fault with them, beyond that they weren't her preferred fighting leathers. With no excuses to do otherwise, Ursula had conceded that particular battle and looked more often the High Queen these days than road-worn warrior princess.

She always looked beautiful to me, so unlike the meek, submissive, and gentle-voiced women of my homeland. In fact, in all my travels, I'd never met another woman like my Essla, another lover of the sword, and as determined as I to wield it for justice.

Just as the first time I'd laid eyes on Ursula, my heart swelled in my chest, filled with the undying love I'd sworn to her service. I'd never regret that I'd given up loyalty and all connection to the blighted homeland of my birth when I'd sworn the *Elskastholrr* to Ursula. That vow—which must be freely given and never requested—had become my compass and foundation.

But I did sometimes wonder how much of the love I felt for her grew from the tattered shreds of guilt and remorse where the love for my sister Jenna had once lived in my heart—and had been ripped away when she disappeared.

In countless small ways, Ursula reminded me of Jenna, whom I'd never forgotten, though I had finally stopped searching for her. I'd kept her existence and fate my personal secret all these years, locked in a box in my heart, where no one could ever open it.

Where the wounds inflicted by the cruel world had nearly killed Jenna before our insane escape attempt, they'd honed Ursula into a weapon. Jenna had possessed no fighting skills, no knowledge of the world outside the Imperial seraglio. Both princesses and heirs to powerful parents, Jenna and Ursula could not be more different.

Perhaps Jenna had survived to go on and find something of Ursula's ferocity. Probably that was a foolish and idealistic hope. Jenna was no doubt dead. Yet I couldn't help wishing otherwise.

"Harlan?" Ursula asked, when I failed to reply to her question. She tipped her head, studying me with a too-knowing gaze, a wealth of other questions crowding her simple asking of my name.

I shook my head, willing the old memories, the miasma of nostalgia—and dread of the future—to go back to the shadows where they belonged. She'd asked me about delegating, a rich question coming from her, who thought she had to handle every cursed thing herself.

"You put me in charge of Ordnung's defenses," I reminded her. "And I'm very good at my job. Let me decide what can be delegated and what requires direct supervision."

She smiled slightly, more of a thin-lipped grimace than anything, as she stepped up to stare out over the walls and the road to the township along with me. "It wasn't a criticism," she replied mildly. "I've received a message from Andi," she said, seeming to change the subject, though I knew this must be why she'd sought the solace of the walls.

"Ah. And how is my heart-sister?" The message held bad news, no doubt, as we seemed to have only that variety of messages lately. And, as Queen of the Tala, Andi lived at the heart of the brewing storm.

Sure enough, Ursula huffed out a sharp, impatient breath, stepping away from me. "Carelessly overextending herself, as usual."

"Sounds like someone else I know," I replied, smiling easily when she glared at me. "I have to point out that you're supposed to be resting before court, not checking up on Ordnung's defenses."

She narrowed her gaze at me, eyes sharpening. "How do you know I didn't come up here looking for you?"

I lifted one shoulder and let it fall. "Did you?"

Giving me that thin-lipped smile, she turned to sweep her gaze over the pastoral scene below us, if one could consider a fully-armed castle with guards at high alert 'pastoral.' "I thought you'd be drilling with the guard," she admitted. She was scrupulous about being honest with me, determined to never again cross lines she thought had nearly destroyed our relationship before. Though I'd explained countless times that nothing could damage my love for her, the rejected and abandoned child who still lived in Ursula's heart would never believe it. All I could do was give her that love without reserve or qualification.

"And before you get annoyed with me," she said, bristling at my expression, "I wasn't checking up on the defenses so much as…" she trailed off, searching for the right words.

"Reassuring yourself that all is as it seems?" I suggested, and held out an arm for her, so she'd lean against me for a bit. She gave me a relieved smile, real affection in it, coming to me with at least that much trust.

"You always understand me—often before I understand myself." She snuggled against me, letting out a long breath. "I hate that the practitioners of Deyrr can mess with our minds. I'm more comfortable with an enemy I can predict. And one I can skewer with my sword."

I hugged her close, her slim form and long bones nearly delicate, though I knew better than most how fast she could strike when provoked, and how lethally. "I do understand—and agree," I told her.

She tipped her head against my cheek, so I kissed her temple, giving her the comfort she'd never ask for, her fiery hair always surprising me with its silky texture. It had grown longer since I'd met her. Tamed for court by her ladies, it lay in sleek waves and ended in wisps down her neck.

"Andi reports that the Tala are gathered and the navy assembled," she returned to her point. "Now that Karyn and Zyr have recovered somewhat from their ordeal, Kiraka has been interrogating them about what they found."

I grunted in sympathy. Kiraka was an old dragon—literally—and as cantankerous as they came.

"It's bad." Ursula said it so softly I almost didn't hear. "Andi expects an attack on Annfwn at any time."

"But the magic barrier is still holding, yes? The Dasnarian navy is still on the other side."

"At last report that seems to be the case, but the ships are massing there as if they expect that to change and soon."

I held her, glad she'd come to me. "We have a lot of might on our side, too. We've done everything we can to prepare."

"I know."

She did. We'd both known most of this. The waiting was what wore on us. She shook herself and stood straight. "Andi warned me to expect attack here. The Deyrr sleepers might have infiltrated deep into all the Thirteen Kingdoms. They're waiting to spring some sort of trap on us all, or they would've attacked already."

"If they do we'll fight back. We're ready for them—and not so easy to surprise."

With a brief smile, she turned back to gaze over her realm. "I wish I could be so sure. Of everything."

Something about the way she said that—some intuition perhaps—sent a brush of alarm that made my short hairs prickle. Something else was on her mind, and it wasn't good.

~ 2 ~

"IT ALL LOOKS so peaceful," she said, gazing out, still skirting the heart of the topic. "So… normal. Like I recall it being back in the day, in Uorsin's early years." She waved a hand to disperse the shades of all that had happened later in the tyrant's rule.

We didn't talk much about her father, the late High King Uorsin, and for good reasons. In fact, it said something that she'd mentioned him voluntarily at all. Just speaking his name put unhappy lines around her mouth, signs that the emotional wounds he'd given her had cracked open to seep pus and old blood. She liked to see herself as whole and healed. I knew her better than that.

I set a hand on the small of her back. Through the flexible silver bodice, Ursula's lean and strong muscles were as tight as I'd anticipated. My Essla is built like a racehorse, all slender speed and alert readiness—and she's equally as high strung. She tried to hide the strain of rule from me, the anxiety she felt for her sisters and her realm, pretending she didn't need me or anyone. Still, she leaned in to my touch. Gratifying, given how long and patiently I'd worked to earn her trust.

"Things were good then, in the early days?" I asked leading-ly, willing to accept this conversation instead of the one that clearly weighed on her.

She frowned slightly, watching something on the road. I followed the line of her attention and found nothing salient, so she must have been seeing images play out in her memories, frowning as she always did when she remembered her father.

"Maybe I just have the idea things were good because he said so all the time," Ursula said slowly. "Uorsin was a great one for singing his own praises. But that's how I remember things, back when Salena was alive, when Andi was still little, and before Ami was born. Abundant and peaceful."

"Those were the years right after the Great War ended," I noted.

She huffed a sigh of acknowledgment. "Exactly, which would play in. If nothing else, Uorsin put a stop to the bloodshed and conflict. He built the roads and mandated that everyone use Common Tongue. In those early years, he accomplished a great deal, and most of the kingdoms prospered. People were relatively happy."

"People think that war stimulates trade," I reflected, "when the underlying truth is that the *end* of war allows trade to rebound."

She nodded, her gaze unfocused, attention still on the past. "I'd come up here to the walls sometimes, just to watch the road and all the people living their lives."

Their normal lives, she meant and didn't have to articulate. "You wouldn't have been ten years old yet," I observed as neutrally as possible. She so rarely spoke of her childhood that I treaded carefully when she did, even when I wasn't certain—as I was now—that she was building up to something else entirely.

"True," she replied, then fell silent, brooding, so I moved fully behind her, working my fingers into the gaps of her bodice to loosen the knots I could reach. She rolled her shoulders with a murmur of relief, and continued. "Truly, back then I came up here mostly to figure out what Andi saw in it. Even at barely four, she had a knack for slipping away from her nurses. We'd always find her up here or on one of the towers, staring out like she'd lost something."

"Was that before she had her bedroom in the tower?"

Ursula flicked me a wry glance over her shoulder. "Yes. The tower bedroom was a solution to the problem of her forever running off. With the views from the windows, she was at least content to stay in her room and look out from there. That changed, of course, once she discovered horses—and proved remarkably good at evading notice to ride off for hours in unpredictable directions. If we'd known then that we were dealing with a budding sorceress, we might've done things differently, but Salena would've been the one to know that and…" she shrugged.

"I might point out that you were but a girl yourself and bore no responsibility for what your mother and father should've handled, as parents and as king and queen."

"There you would be wrong. Taking care of Andi and Ami was always my responsibility, whether they liked it or not. And the Thirteen are my responsibility." Her face hardened, and she turned to face me. "You're worried about something. That's why you keep coming up here. But not about war. What aren't you telling me?"

I shouldn't have been surprised at what she noticed. Even apparently and thoroughly preoccupied with matters of court and defense, Ursula missed very little. "This is simply a good place to think," I hedged, hoping that might be enough to deflect her.

She leaned back against the parapet, facing me with crossed arms. "You think and think, yet you never tell me what plagues your thoughts. Don't you think it's about time you changed that?"

"You don't need to worry about me," I told her, a weak defense, but I didn't have a better one.

She laughed, short and without humor. "First, that's not true. Second, I do worry because I love you, and I'm reliably informed that it's not only natural to worry about the people we love, it's usually expected. Third, that reply was an evasion."

I raised an eyebrow at her. I might've left the Imperial Palace of Dasnaria far behind in my misbegotten past, but I'd been around plenty of rulers in a variety of lands and I knew how to handle an irritated monarch. More, I knew Ursula. Better than I knew my own heart. "You have plenty on your mind and I can handle myself."

"Another evasion," she shot back. Debating with Ursula often felt the same as sparring with her, though it was rarely as enjoyable since the odds of getting my hands on her were much lower in a debate.

My own irritation rising to meet hers, I gave her a long, very calm look. "I appreciate that you love me enough to worry about me, but it's simply old memories plaguing me, like a bad joint that aches when the weather changes."

"Tell me anyway." She raised her brows in challenge, but her voice held an almost pleading note.

Uncertain of my footing, I wondered where this was going. She didn't usually press like this. "Essla, there are things my vows prohibit me from speaking of. I can't tell you."

Her winged eyebrows lowered, forking into a dark frown. "Those vows again." She spat the words as if they were distasteful.

"Those vows again," I agreed. I found I'd folded my own arms in a mirror of hers, unconsciously harmonizing with her even when she pissed me off. Too late to undo it without tipping her off. "They are nothing important, especially compared to your other concerns. My secrets have nothing to do with the security of your realm. You needn't be concerned that I would keep something from you that you need to know."

Her frown cleared, leaving her expression carefully blank, though her lips parted slightly to draw in a quick breath before she firmed her mouth and her gaze went steely. "I see," she replied in a neutral tone. "I suppose I'd foolishly believed I could listen to your worries as you've so often listened to mine. I apologize for my presumption." She stood to go.

I cursed myself. I'd hurt her, thoughtlessly and clumsily. Putting a hand on her arm, I stopped her. "Essla, I'm sorry."

She stared past me, her throat working as she swallowed whatever words sprang to her lips. When her gaze met mine, her eyes had gone silvery with the sheen of tears she'd never permit herself to shed. "We're all growing further apart—have you noticed? Dafne is preoccupied with her pregnancy and translating for Kiraka. Ami is ensconced at Windroven with her lover and the children—I'll never pry her out of there."

"And Andi?" I prompted. Of everyone, I knew Ursula missed Andi the most.

"More like our mother every day," she replied, weary affection in her voice. "Of us all, she's carrying the heaviest burden, so I do my best not to add to it. Everyone is devoting themselves to preparing for this war. We all know that Annfwn will be where Deyrr attacks. And here I sit in Ordnung, doing nothing, far away from it all."

"You're hardly doing nothing." I could only wish she'd do a bit less. "You wake before dawn and rarely go to sleep before midnight."

She shook her head, studying her boots. "All meetings and talk, talk, talk. I've lost most of my Hawks to other duties—Jepp and Marskal off fighting the battles I used to."

I understood what she meant. She and I, both creatures of action, accustomed to leading from the front. But being High Queen meant she'd had to return to Castle Ordnung and direct strategy from safe inside walls. As for me, my Vervaldr had all been released from their contracts, some almost certainly returned to Dasnaria, while others were absorbed into Ordnung's guard, or dispersed into other parts of the troops we had amassed in defense of the Thirteen Kingdoms.

Though I'd taken over for the unfortunate Lord Percy, one of the first victims of Deyrr's occupation of Ordnung and former Captain of the Guard, I had no real title or role. I wasn't fool enough to believe that I could ever be more than Ursula's unofficial consort, nor did that bother me. That was the nature of the vows I'd given her, to support her in any way I could.

That also meant keeping her safe.

"You're needed here," I told her, emphasizing what she already knew. "You're too important to risk on the front lines of this fight."

"I know that in my head. My heart is another matter." She took a deep breath, uncharacteristic vulnerability in her eyes when she met my gaze. "Speaking of which, I didn't expect you to disappear on me."

The vague dread coalesced, sharpening into wary surprise that she'd say such a thing. "I'm right here," I said, and turned her so she faced me, squeezing both shoulders so she'd feel it.

"Are you sure?" She studied me, emotion banished, all keen observation. "You haven't been the same since my injury."

Shocked, I let go of her, sudden cold numbing my fingers nerveless. The events of that terrible day flooded back in excruciating and vivid detail. The heat of the tropical sun and the pitch of the Tala ship beneath my boots, rocking in the gentle waves. The eerie silence and the sharp scent of blood, raw meat, and entrails spilling from Ursula when the High Priestess gutted her. How I stood there frozen, helpless, unable to move in the slightest. All those years I'd built my strength, honed my skills, to make myself into warrior enough to protect the woman I loved and it had all been for nothing.

I hadn't been able to protect Ursula any more than I'd been able to save Jenna. Fury and fear warred in me.

"Your *injury?*" I sneered the word, unreasonable rage firing in me that she could speak of it so casually. "Let's rephrase for accuracy. You mean when you very nearly *died*." So pale and weak in my arms when she collapsed, her blood pooling on the deck around us. If not for magical healing, she *would* have died there. For long moments, I'd been sure she was gone. And I'd been helpless to do anything about it.

A flare of unhappy triumph crossed Ursula's face. She was too much the warrior not to be pleased with her accurate piercing of my emotional armor, and too much the woman who loved me not to be sorry about it. "I didn't die."

"It was a near thing… *and* you're still not totally healed."

She opened her mouth to protest and I cut her off with a chop of my hand through the air. "Don't lie to me," I bit out. "You don't have your former strength and speed. Your color still isn't right, and you won't *get* better when you work yourself to the bone and refuse to rest."

"My kingdom faces attack from a two-pronged enemy, either of which could devastate us entirely on its own, and they've joined forces. I've been betrayed from within, I'm still new to my throne and utterly out of my depth. I can't afford to rest."

"I understand that," I ground out. "But you can't afford not to rest. If you don't care about yourself, at least think about the people who love you."

"I love you, too," she replied seriously. "Because of that, I'm suggesting that whatever is going on inside your head is getting to you. Normally you're very good at leaving the past where it belongs, but lately you're letting it eat away at you. You were the one to teach me that ignoring emotional wounds weakens us. If you won't talk to me about it, then find someone else to listen."

I scrubbed my hands over my scalp, willing my brain to kick in with a reply to soothe her. "I just worry about you is all," I said. "There's nothing else that needs discussing."

"Like I worry about you?" She parried.

"No." I called on the meditative calm of the *Skablykrr* that had always served me so well, but couldn't grasp it, my hand groping in the mental dark and coming up empty. "That's different," I threw out, a poor defense and we both knew it.

"Is it?" she asked coolly, neatly knocking that aside and leaving me open.

I had no answer, nothing else to offer. She dipped her chin in wry acknowledgement, then shrugged it off. "You're a stubborn man, Harlan, and I've got other things to do this morning than bash my head against this particular wall."

She put her hand to her sword and took a few steps, then changed her mind and turned back to me, a certain resolve in the line of her jaw.

I knew that look well, though it usually meant she'd decided to draw a metaphorical dagger she'd hidden up her sleeve in dealing with a recalcitrant ambassador or courtier—and the strike of that hidden weapon would inevitably be devastating. Though I'd seen her use it on others, she'd never turned it on me. She'd softened me up, deflecting and tiring me, all in preparation for this particular blow.

She scanned the immediate area, checking that the guards still gave us privacy, making sure her battlefield remained clear.

I braced myself. This would hurt.

"I know about Jenna," she said.

~ 3 ~

NO AMOUNT OF bracing could've prepared me for that.

Hearing the name I hadn't spoken—or heard anyone else speak—in over twenty years fall from Ursula's lips shocked me as little else could. She'd timed her attack perfectly, distracting me by evoking the fear for her that plagued me, outmaneuvering me, then slipping under my guard to deliver that strike directly to my heart.

She watched me with keen attention, no doubt cataloguing every whisper of reaction. I'd had to fall in love with a woman with an intellect as razor sharp as her sword. I should've known she'd ferret out my secrets eventually.

Even those I'd vowed to keep, because they weren't only mine.

"How?" I finally managed to ask, once I had the breath to sound reasonably in control of myself. "Kral told you," I realized, my thoughts finally catching up.

My brother Kral had unexpectedly defected to our side of the war, becoming the only member of my family I didn't have to dread facing on a battlefield. He also formed the third point of our lethal family triangle: Kral, Jenna, and me. The bad blood had festered between us for years until we agreed to put it away. Not that we'd actually dealt with it. I'd thought he didn't care to discuss it any more than I did.

"Not Kral." Ursula replied, confirming that. "He's as tight-lipped on the topic as you are. Jepp told me."

"Jepp," I echoed, feeling thick and stupid. Former scout in Ursula's elite troop of Hawks, Jepp had inexplicably fallen in love with my domineering and arrogant brother, and was the reason he'd left the Empire. She didn't give up her footloose ways and settle down—she hadn't changed that dramatically—instead she sailed the seas with Kral on his ship the *Hákyrling*. And Ursula had restored Kral's title and status as General, but of our forces in the field. The *Hákyrling* was patrolling the magic barrier, watching for incursions from Deyrr and monitoring the build-up of the Dasnarian navy.

Surely Jepp hadn't learned about Jenna from Kral. Ah… but, Jepp had gone to Dasnaria as a spy. She'd been to the Imperial Palace.

Acutely aware of Ursula's scrutiny as I put it together, I sat, the weight of the past and the secrets I'd carried so long suddenly feeling too heavy to bear. "Jepp learned the story in Dasnaria." I nodded to myself when Ursula's expression confirmed it. "Who told her?"

"Your *other* sisters, Inga and Helva—more sisters I had no idea existed—told her the whole story. She reported it to me."

I winced, rubbing my eyes with one hand, bracing myself on the wall with the other, as I felt oddly dizzy. Of course Jepp had reported everything to her captain and queen. "How long have you known?"

Ursula's mouth thinned, not pleased with that response. Truly I was lucky she hadn't cut my throat in my sleep. The last time she'd discovered I'd kept a secret from her about my family—that I was a former prince of the imperial household in Dasnaria—she'd drawn blood, then coolly cut me out of her life. Not that she'd had much luck with that. As she'd noted, I could be a stubborn man.

"I debriefed Jepp on the Tala ship while I was recovering from my *injury*." She raised a brow, daring me to quibble with the term again. I wouldn't. I needed to pick my battles with her very carefully now.

I nodded, assimilating all of it. That had happened months ago. All this time, Ursula had known and said nothing. I could take comfort that she'd continued to share my bed and welcomed me with her body, but I could see now that we hadn't been quite the same—and that I'd been too preoccupied to notice.

"It seems then that the distance between us isn't entirely of my own making," I said, more of a feint than a strike, just to test her defenses.

Her jaw tightened, her thumb caressing the faceted ruby in the hilt of her sword. "I'm right here," she said, tossing my words back at me. "And I've given you plenty of opportunities to tell me all of this. Including just a moment ago."

She had, I realized, asking me all those leading questions about my family, about the bad blood between me and Kral. Asking me to confide my worries in her. And I'd deflected them all, out of habit, in part. Also out of the comfortable assumption that she didn't know that history. Over time it had been easier not to talk about *any* of the sisters I'd left behind, when I talked about Dasnaria at all. That's the great problem with lies of omission—over time, they begin to feel less like lies than an alternate truth, one that becomes a façade that weakens with age.

Because I hadn't replied, she continued. "Jepp explained that these vows of yours are related to this family history, so I should give you latitude for that—in fact, she thought long and hard whether to tell *me* everything she knew—but I've had a lot of time, and enforced inactivity, to contemplate this and I think there's a lot you could have confided in me, had you chosen to."

I couldn't argue with that. The fact that Jepp had considered not reporting everything she knew… that would've lodged in Ursula's heart, and craw, as well. I'd well and truly fucked this up.

I spread my hands, making myself meet her penetrating gaze. "I apologize. I'm at fault and I don't expect forgiveness."

She stared at me, unrelenting. "You do that so easily, but I don't think this is that simple for me."

"I'm surprised you haven't tried to kill me," I ventured, trying for the joke.

"I thought about it," she answered crisply, but without her usual fire. Then she looked away. "I don't understand why you wouldn't at least tell me about Inga and Helva. *Brothers.* You only ever mentioned brothers. You know *everything* about me—things no other living person does, because you wouldn't settle for anything less—and you didn't trust me with the smallest thing. All I can think about is what else I don't know about you. I'm not at all sure where to go from here."

"Court should be starting soon," I offered, still hoping for levity. The other possibility, that I'd destroyed her trust in me, didn't bear thinking about. Ursula didn't trust easily. What another woman might be able to forgive and forget would feel like the ultimate betrayal to her.

She leveled an icy glare on me. "As you so love to say, they can hardly start without me."

I braced my hands on my thighs, studying them. "Why to-day?" I asked.

"Excuse me?" She'd drawn her High Queen imperious atti-tude around herself like a protective cloak, the offense clear in her voice. When I looked at her, she'd indeed straightened her spine, looking every inch the warrior queen.

I barreled on, eager to at least extract myself from this corner she'd boxed me into. Standing, I gestured to the heights of Ordnung's walls, arguably one of the very few places we could speak without being interrupted or overheard by the ubiquitous staff and anxious courtiers who plagued every moment of Ursula's day. She'd picked this spot and plotted her attack, meticulously planned and devastatingly thorough.

"Why did you choose today to confront me with this, when you've known for months?" I clarified. "You could've told me you knew long before this, instead of asking leading questions, testing me. You let me hang as you reeled in the rope."

"Don't you dare try to turn this back on me," she warned, quiet fury in her tone, her fingers sliding down to curl around the hilt of her sword. She stood just outside my reach, were I to draw my own broadsword on her—a distance she knew precisely from all the times we'd sparred.

"Will you draw on me?" I asked softly. I didn't think she would. We'd come a long way with each other, and she'd promised never pull a weapon on me again. Not a physical one, anyway, or rather, not with lethal intent. But my Essla was a woman of strong passions and not always predictable. I could best her with my strength where she outmatched me in speed.

I, however, could never harm her. Not physically. In her righteous anger, she might have no such scruples with me.

"I'm tempted," she replied.

"Then do it," I dared her. Better to fight it out and get it done.

"You'd like that, wouldn't you?" Then she sagged, releasing her blade and lifting her hands to her face. "It would be *easier*. I'm aware that's one of the ways you manage me."

Reflexively, I stepped toward her, to comfort her, to—

"Don't." Her hard voice cut me short. She dropped her

hands and gazed at me. "To answer your question, two reasons why today. The first…" Her voice shook as it never did, and she firmed her jaw. "I think I couldn't stand it anymore. I promised you a long time ago that I wouldn't walk away again without letting you explain, but I waited every day for you to tell me about this—even pieces of it—and day after day you pretended it wasn't there, carving a hole between us. Yes, it would be easier to call you out, to match blades and see who takes first blood, but that would be redundant. First blood is yours. This cut me, Harlan. Cut me to the quick and I'm still bleeding."

"Essla, I'm sorry," I said, fully realizing the weakness of those words, how ineffective to express anything at all.

"I'm sure you are." She smiled slightly, but it didn't touch the sorrow in her eyes. "And I wish that could be enough for me. Maybe it's a flaw in my character, but it isn't enough. There aren't that many people in my life I can believe will always tell me the truth—now more than ever. You were one of those people."

The past tense hit me like a knife to the kidneys, and I groped for breath to reply.

"You have a choice, I think," she continued. "The second reason is that starting two weeks ago I received a series of messages from Dasnaria, relaying information supposedly leaked from the Imperial Palace."

I grappled with that equally astonishing news—as well as the fact that she'd kept it from me. "How do you know that's where it's from?" I asked.

"I don't have a way of verifying, do I?" She snapped. "The information is coded to make me think it comes from someone in your family. 'From inside the fist,' it said."

The stunning blows kept coming. That would indeed imply from a Konyngrr—the silver fist being our family emblem—as

Ursula knew, but few others would.

"If it's legitimate, I think the messages come from one or both of your sisters."

"My sisters?" I echoed, pondering the absolute implausibility of that.

"Aspects of the messages are decidedly feminine. What are the odds it's them—or perhaps another female *associate* of yours?" she pressed. "What can you tell me without violating your *vows*?"

"I…" I didn't know what to say. Mostly I wanted to fight back, to growl at her not to interrogate me like one of her subjects—especially that jab about some unknown female associate—even as I knew I deserved every bit of it. "It's not easy to untangle those threads, what I can and can't reveal. That's why I never mentioned any of my sisters, because it was easier to put everything about them behind the same door."

She nodded slightly, unsurprised. "I think you have to consider that your loyalties are divided. We face a war with your family and—"

"There is no question that my loyalty lies with you," I interrupted her furiously.

She held up a hand, icily calm. Quite the reversal for us. "I've given this a lot of thought," she reminded me. "You need to do the same. You've withheld information from me that's arguably critical to this impending war. I know you want to believe that the *Elskastholrr* you swore to me makes everything clear cut, but you have other vows, too, ones you made before that to keep your sisters secret. Which vows take precedence, Harlan?"

Flummoxed, I had no reply. I didn't need one, evidently, because she nodded again, smiling sadly. "There is no easy way out of this," she repeated. "If you have to leave in order to reconcile your conflicting interests, I'll understand."

Leave? The thought of leaving her shredded my heart. "How can you even think I would?" I asked, my voice coming out ragged. "Or could?"

"We always knew our love affair might be short-lived," she replied, softly, with deep sorrow. "That our differences might end at exactly this sort of conflict. I told you from the beginning that I belonged to the High Throne first, and because of that I'm a warrior for my kingdom, and only incidentally a woman."

"And I told you that's only because you don't put the woman first," I said with more bitterness than I'd intended.

"You're absolutely right." She inclined her chin, acknowledging the problem, but not apologizing. "I don't put the woman first. I can't, and I never will. I don't want you to leave. You'll tear my heart out and take it with you if you go. But I belonged to the High Throne from the day of my birth, and I can't let you stay if you're a threat to it."

~ 4 ~

S HATTERED, I WATCHED her stride away. The guards came to attention, saluting as she passed, the warm breeze catching the long coattail skirts of the black velvet gown, making them snap like the tower pennants, the silver of the leggings flashing in the cuts, black boots making crisp sounds now that she wasn't being stealthy. She looked long, lean, and as dangerous as her sword.

How cleanly she'd cut out my heart, taking it with her and leaving me hollow.

Every muscle and nerve in my body urged me to run after her. To say what, though? In her usual fashion, Ursula had sliced to the bones of the problem. I'd never thought of my loyalties as divided, but they were. With another woman, that wouldn't matter. The way we felt about each other would outweigh everything else. Another woman wouldn't allow a matter of principle to override her heart.

But then, I hadn't fallen in love with another woman.

It had only ever been Ursula for me, and always would be—despite those past vows.

Pledging the *Elskastholrr* to her had been an easy decision. I'd been a simpler person then. A mercenary captain, disinherited from my past. The secrets I'd carried hadn't been so heavy, and it had been easy—that word again—to let them lie buried. Easy at that time to forget I'd ever been anyone else.

In its purest form, the *Elskastholrr* exists only in the heart and mind of the one who vows it. Ursula, heir to the throne of a tyrant, beloved of her people and obvious choice as their savior, had been a fine recipient for my vow. After witnessing the abuse of power in far too many forms and places, I had no desire to be king, but I would happily serve as kingmaker. In that crystal moment of decision, I saw a scenario where I'd serve out my vows and Ursula would never know about the *Elskastholrr*.

Deceptively simple.

I had told her, eventually, because she'd asked—and because I'd been unable to resist the temptation to have her. Nothing had remained simple for me after that. And, now, like the undead creatures animated by Deyrr's cursed magic, the events of the past trudged relentlessly forward to convene with the present.

There is no easy way out of this. Ursula had the right of it. Even if I could mark the boundaries of the vows in my mind, tell her everything but the essentials I'd sworn in blood and flesh never to reveal, the secrets I kept would still lie festering between us.

When I pledged the *Elskastholrr* to Ursula, I hadn't given those other, older vows I'd taken to protect Jenna a second thought. I'd had no expectation that Ursula would become my lover, that she'd return my love. A mercenary in love with a princess—nothing should have come of it.

Kral had himself a good laugh about it when he found out. Though with his practical, ambitious nature, he'd always thought the *Elskastholrr* a hopelessly romantic and self-destructive tradition anyway. He'd never see his way to being so selfless that he'd pledge himself to a woman for the rest of his life, whether she returned his regard or not. Though Jepp may have changed that. She wouldn't want eternal devotion so much, but she *would* demand commitment—at knife point, if necessary.

Being honest with myself, I'd have to admit that I'd embraced the hopeless, even punitive aspects of pledging myself to an impossible love. Though I'd pursued Ursula, I hadn't hoped for more than a night or two in her bed to sustain me. *We always knew our love affair might be short-lived.* I huffed out a laugh, a despairing edge to it that made a nearby guard look at me sharply.

I hadn't known that she hadn't had any real lovers before—or that in enticing her to unfurl her tightly closed heart, I'd become the sole caretaker of her intimate self.

Ursula would say this is why I shouldn't have vowed myself to her without even having a conversation first. She'd have a fair point, too, except that I suspected we could've conversed for years and I wouldn't have learned what I needed to know.

I knew I could spend the rest of my life with her and not be able to predict where her canny mind would go next.

Knowing her as I did now, however, how things had fallen out between us was all too predictable. I'd breached her walls and found my way to the heart of her as no one else had. Ursula didn't trust or love easily, but when she did, she committed herself entirely, with unflagging loyalty and determination.

Her own version of the *Elskastholrr*, in a way.

I had no doubt that if I did leave, she'd never give her heart again. She might eventually agree to a marriage, perhaps even take another man to her bed to produce an heir of her own body for the High Throne and the realm she loved above all else. But she was the kind to give her heart only once. Another way that she and I were the same.

From the beginning I'd been cognizant that if we succeeded in putting her on the High Throne, she'd one day make a marriage of state and not to me, a foreign mercenary. I would handle that eventuality when it happened—though the thought of another man making love to my Essla filled me with protective fury.

How could another man understand her particular fragility? Especially since she hid it so well under that tough skin and slicing wit. She'd be so easy to injure. If she succeeded in sending me away, and she married another, I wouldn't even be there to help her through that painful transition.

No matter what, I needed to make sure I stayed. I'd have to do what I could to bridge this chasm I'd created.

The great irony was that the vows I'd taken no longer served any real purpose. I couldn't reveal where Jenna had gone, because I didn't know. I'd once had guesses. We'd planned to flee together to Halabahna, to see the elephants, but I'd looked for her there and never found a trace of her.

Elephants. Had Jenna ever found them? For a long time I'd thought if I looked where elephants are, I'd eventually find her, but no.

I had to face that she'd probably died long ago. Or been captured, enslaved. An extraordinarily beautiful young woman with no ability to defend herself… It was a mark of my foolish idealism that I could even entertain anything but the worst fears for her fate. I'd likely never know what happened to her—and that I'd kept these heavy, destructive secrets all this time for no reason at all.

An alarmed shout went up from the lookout.

I spun, drawing my broadsword as I did, gratified that my sweeping glance verified all the guards in sight did likewise, brandishing whatever weapons they used best. The shout came from the highest tower, from a young woman I knew to be one of Jepp's protégées, a scout for the Hawks. She waved a flag in a complicated series of dips and twirls—one of their cryptic codes

I had yet to learn—and I scanned for the nearest Hawk commander. Brant. With a gesture I summoned him and he came at a run.

"Report," I ordered.

He turned to watch the flag. "Unidentified movement. Request to be alert. Shadows in motion."

Shadows in motion. "Nothing more?"

Brant shook his head, eyes still on the lookout. "Message is repeating. I'll go see if I can find out more from Dary."

I grunted acknowledgement, scanning the shadows in question. The bright summer morning left few enough of them, but corners of the courtyard remained filled with deep shade cast by the high walls. I saw nothing unusual—certainly nothing to swing my sword at—but Ursula's Hawks weren't given to flights of fancy or false alarms.

With the enemy we faced, formless and born of darkest magics, anything odd could be an attack. Far better to err on the side of caution. Ursula was right that Annfwn was the apparent focus of Deyrr's enmity, but Ordnung remained the capital of the Thirteen Kingdoms. Deyrr wanted the heart of magic, but Emperor Hestar would want the High Throne. Because the two had joined forces, anything could happen.

Still, I felt more and more like a fool, seeing nothing strange or alarming, pointing my sword at shadows. We all did, bristling with weapons and anxiety, while the merry sounds of trade and a fine summer morning rang out from the road and township.

A metaphor for my current situation if ever there was one.

"Captain." Brant returned from conferring with Dary. "Recommend we stand down from high alert but increase eyes on the situation. Dary saw something she can't explain—like smoke or fog in the shadows—but it hasn't recurred. She asked me to relay her apologies for a false alarm, which I will, though I don't think they're necessary. She's as sharp-eyed as they come and solid with it."

"No," I replied, sheathing my broadsword and rubbing a hand over the back of my neck where the hair prickled with chill foreboding, even as the sun made my skin slick with sweat. "No apologies for a report made in earnest. Call on whoever you need to help watch. Dogs, too."

"Dary suggested some of the hunting falcons, as they're good with picking out small movements in bright daylight."

"Do it." He saluted and I returned it, then went to report the incident to the woman currently considering kicking me out of her bed—and her life.

When I reached the throne room, Ursula had already convened court and sat on the High Throne. The setup had changed since the early days when I first arrived with my Vervaldr, hired by Ursula's father to shore up what I quickly understood to be his mad and crumbling grip on power. In those days he'd sat on an iron throne flanked by four others, all empty.

One had been vacant for twelve years, once belonging to Salena, the dead sorceress queen, and the other three to her daughters, all away from Ordnung for various reasons. I'd thought I'd grown open-minded since leaving Dasnaria, but I'd been astonished to learn Uorsin's heir was his eldest daughter, an unmarried woman.

When she returned home, striding down the center aisle of court, covered in road dust, eyes steely with resolve, and proceeded to engage in a battle of wits with her father… well, I'd understood. And fallen hard.

Unlike Ursula that day, I didn't approach the High Throne down the center aisle, but took the long way around the assembled courtiers, keeping to the shadows in my own way, I supposed. It bothered Ursula far more than it did me that I had no official place in her court. As the youngest of seven legitimate sons born to my father, I'd been a prince in the Imperial Palace, sure, but one largely ignored in favor of those with a far greater chance of becoming emperor. When I'd been a boy that had rankled.

Discovering the kind of lives my sisters led had given me sorely needed perspective on just how fortunate I'd been.

When I reached my usual post at the side and foot of Ursula's throne, she gave me a narrow glance from the side of her flinty eyes. "I didn't expect you here," she murmured.

"It's where I belong," I replied simply, repeating a truth I'd had to drum into her thick skull. Folding my arms, I settled into the relaxed stance I could maintain for hours—and often did when court dragged on for a ridiculously long time. So determined not to repeat her father's mistakes, Ursula rarely cut off the petitions when any rational person would. Another consequence of her being away from Ordnung for so long—the business of the kingdoms, major and ridiculously minor, had piled up. The King of Carienne, Groningen, had handled a great deal of it as regent in her absence, but many people held onto their petitions, awaiting the return of the High Queen, certain they merited her personal attention.

In my opinion, very few of their urgent requests truly rose to that level. But that was another difference between my homeland and this realm. In Dasnaria, His Imperial Majesty the Emperor would never trouble himself with such trivia. He relied on his nobility to govern, which inevitably led to corruption and abuse of power.

Surely there had to be a middle ground between the two extremes.

Ursula delivered her decision on the current question. While Shua—the cleric who'd taken on Dafne's role—shuffled documents and prepared to call the next petitioner, Ursula flicked another glance at me. "What's wrong?" she wanted to know.

When I gave her a placid, questioning look, she made an impatient sound and gestured me to approach. "I know the difference between you being pissed at me and there being something of concern. Tell me what happened."

~ **5** ~

THUS OFFICIALLY SUMMONED, I stepped up the dais to her throne. When she'd removed the vacant thrones, she'd replaced the imposing and unyielding one of her father's with a wooden one that gave a nod to the other half of her heritage. A gift from the Tala, it had been created from wood and magic. Not carved, but grown into its shape, the mahogany hardwood flowed without seam or nail, a bloodred nearly black, into the form of spread hawk's wings. The arms and feet of the great chair echoed talons and the winged back provided a striking frame for the High Queen's imposing presence.

By staying one level below her, I observed protocol and avoided appearing to loom over her. "Nothing urgent," I replied. "Dary spotted something strange in the shadows, but it seemed to disappear again."

Ursula considered that with interest. Even now she knew all of her Hawks by name. "Dary has sharp eyes. Almost as good as Jepp. Still it would be helpful to augment the watch with some of the shapeshifters Andi promised to send."

"We're bringing in dogs and falcons," I reported, "but supplementing with shapeshifter eyes would be ideal."

She considered me. "Perhaps you could travel to Annfwn with the message. Andi might take that more seriously."

I caught and held her gaze, delicately setting my mental feet on the narrow line between subject and lover. "Don't send me away."

"Would you go if I ordered it?" She sounded idly curious. And didn't fool me for a moment.

I simply saluted her with the *Elskastholrr*, not with a blade—even I didn't draw on the High Throne—but with two fingers against my forehead in lieu of a blade. The essence of the vow is in the physical demonstration and, indeed, no words go with it. The intent lies entirely in the heart and mind.

She read it in me with a flicker of resignation, and broke her gaze away to the patiently waiting courtiers. "As you were," she told me, the quiet words speaking volumes.

I'd returned to my place and she to the business of the realm, when the warning bells sounded from the walls. First-level alert. The courtiers erupted into shouts of panic.

Drawing my broadsword, I positioned myself in front of the throne, scanning the room for signs of attack before glancing back at Ursula, who'd leapt to her feet, her own sword in hand. "You know the drill, Your Majesty," I declared loudly enough for all nearby to hear.

Members of Ordnung's guard and Ursula's Hawks, a protective cadre I'd personally chosen, formed a circle around the throne, more running into the room.

She glared at me in impotent fury, but in this situation our hierarchy reversed itself. As much as she might resent it, the focus of Ordnung's response to attack had to be protecting the High Queen. We'd fought about it at length—usually with most stimulating results—and she'd at last conceded responsibility to me in a state of emergency.

Satisfied with her protection, I nodded at the ranking commander. "If you don't hear the all-clear, take Her Majesty to the safe room."

She saluted in the Hawk's style, fist over heart.

"Harlan!" Ursula's voice cut through the chaos.

I looked to her, braced for argument, but she set her jaw. "Be careful."

"Always." I grinned at her, her exasperated glare giving me heart, then took off running down the center aisle, courtiers scurrying still to both clear the way and move closer to safety. One part of my mind—the part that had made the Vervaldr the best mercenary troop a fortune could buy—noted what worked in our emergency plan and what didn't.

Courtiers, curse the lot of them, acted more like terrified chickens than anything. A few, the savvy and those experienced in the conflicts that had shaken their kingdoms over the last years, handled the crisis with efficient, even cynical calm. Most, however, had gone straight into panic and hindered the rest.

Next time—if we had a next time—I'd have troops assigned to crowd control. The former dungeons, now a growing library, made for excellent safe rooms. The deepest and most difficult to access was reserved for Ursula and the best of her elite guards, but no reason the courtiers couldn't be sent directly to the rooms that ringed it. More buffer against the enemy reaching the High Queen.

A grim smile stretched my lips as I shouldered a panicked young diplomat aside, his pile of scrolls scattering across the floor, and I imagined him giving his life to protect his liege.

The savage fantasy helped vent my frustration. Truly Ursula should be in the safe room already, but—as with all things to do with her—I'd also eventually compromised. She'd successfully convinced me that it would make her look weak if she ran and hid at the first alarm, but she'd promised to go at the second-level bells, or in the absence of an all clear. Theoretically.

I'd believe it when I saw her do it. She refused to drill in worst case scenarios.

My own handpicked team fell in behind me as I barreled out of the throne room and into the formal courtyard of the castle. Composed of Vervaldr, Hawks, and a few others, these fighters all either augmented my own strengths or compensated for my weaknesses. At least, those weaknesses I could do anything about. The biggest one should be in a safe room and wasn't.

Deliberately, I cleared my mind, reciting the mantras of the *Skablykyrr*, the ancient words tolling in my mind and driving out everything else. I needed to fight and kill, to do and be nothing else but the intelligence behind my blade.

Taking the fastest route, I climbed the ladder to the walls, peripherally aware of the precision teams who raised the ladders for my comrades to climb, then lowered them again. We'd been able to drill *that* much.

Brant awaited me as I topped the wall. "Dragon, Captain. Approaching from the west." He pointed and I followed the line of his finger.

A densely dark flying creature flew steadily toward us. With the long-winged silhouette of a vulture, it seemed to be no bigger than that—until I mentally measured it against the mountains. Enormous. Still distant, but rapidly gaining.

"Sand at the ready?" I jogged beside Brant.

"Yes. And water."

"Water won't work on dragon fire. Neither will arrows. Save those. Use the ballistae."

"Already armed and waiting for range."

I didn't know if we could do much damage to an attacking dragon on the wing, but we'd certainly find out. We reached the guard station below the lookout tower. Dary was still up there, using her flag in crisp, unhurried communication. "Get Dary down," I told him.

"Sir, if there's another—"

"If there's an attack from another direction, it will be nothing compared to dragon fire. Get her down. Everyone not on the ballistae takes cover."

He saluted and obeyed, signaling to Dary and passing along my orders. I squinted at the dragon, growing ever larger, like a slowly falling star whose explosive landing could likely make Ordnung into a crater. The words itched to jump out, to order the second-level warning bell rung, but I couldn't be sure yet—and Ursula wouldn't easily forgive a false alarm.

On the one hand, all the living dragons we knew of were friendly. On the other, I'd seen firsthand what Kiraka, one of those "friendly" dragons, had done to Ursula's Tala cousin Zynda. She'd been immolated and survived only by magic and possibly—literally—divine intervention.

I stared at it, willing my eyes to see more than they did. I beckoned to Dary. "Is the dragon a bronze color?" I demanded.

"No, Captain. Black, or very deep blue. Hard to tell at this distance with the light the way it is."

I nodded, biting down on the frustration. Dary had good eyes indeed if she could see that much—and she must've picked out that it was a dragon, not a bird, when it had been merely a speck in the distance, given its rate of approach.

Kiraka was bronze, so that ruled her out. And the friendly dragon liberated from under the dormant volcano at Windroven was silver. At least they did us the favor of being different colors, much good may it do us.

Compared to the bedlam indoors, the walls were eerily silent. The township, alert to the bells of Ordnung, had gone quiet as everyone took shelter. Even the traffic on the trade road had halted, horses and oxen unharnessed and taken to cover, people crouching under wagons where necessary. The courtiers could learn from them.

Otherwise the quiet was broken only by the snap of Ordnung's pennants in the wind, and the occasional scrape of a foot or weapon as we waited in tense readiness to fight an unstoppable enemy. One pass of dragon fire could wipe out half the soldiers on the wall.

"Track that aim," I called out as the dragon veered from its direct approach. The crews on the ballistae were ahead of me, using the swivel mounts to good purpose. The dragon swung east, banking with spread wings on a glide, its massive shadow passing over us as its bulk blocked the sun.

"Nearly in range," the near-end ballista crew leader called.

"There's a rider," Dary called out from her perch standing atop the parapet. Not at all under cover but at least not so easy a target as on the lookout tower.

I squinted at the dragon, barely making out a figure on its back. If it was one of the Deyrr sorcerers, they could wipe our minds and make us happy to die by dragon fire.

"Correction." Dary had a hand up, ticking fingers to show three. "Multiple riders."

"Count of five to range," the crew leader announced.

"Stand by to launch," I ordered, starting the countdown in my head.

"Rider appears to be signaling," Dary called.

Four.

"Can you make it out?" Brant asked.

"Not easy at this distance, sir."

Three.

"Could be spellcasting," I warned.

"Best guess," Brant ordered. "Now."

Two.

Dary's face was pinched in concentration. I didn't know how

she could see anything. "On my signal," I told the ballista crew.

One.

"We have the target, Captain."

"Wait!" Dary nearly leapt off the parapet. "It's Lieutenant Marskal."

"Are you sure?" Brant snapped.

"His personal signal, sir." She did leap off the parapet, running up to me, dark eyes large in her tight face. "Don't shoot, Captain. I'd stake my life on it."

"Stand down," I ordered the ballistae crews, who leapt to disarm the weapons. "But keep the alert. You're staking the lives of everyone in Ordnung, Dary—not just yours."

"Yes, sir." She spun to watch the dragon as they closed the distance, no doubt having observed our disarming. Then she pumped a fist in the sky. "It *is* him. And Scout Jepp and General Kral."

This day got better and better. At least we wouldn't die by dragon fire.

"Stand down to normal alert," I called. "And send for Her Majesty. I'll meet her at the castle gates. She'll no doubt want to see this."

~ 6 ~

H ER SWORD SHEATHED at her hip, tri-point crown glinting, and a phalanx of her personal guard trailing, Ursula strode through the outer gates, sharp gaze fixing on me for a long, inscrutable moment before she scanned the scene. Without a flicker of surprise, she took in the unprecedented sight of the enormous blue-black dragon gently wafting to settle on the expanse where tradesfolk and visitors to Castle Ordnung typically pastured their horses. Defying all common sense, the immense creature hovered like a hummingbird, setting itself down precisely and gently, though the great leathery wings stirred dust into whirlwinds.

"Who is it?" Ursula inquired, as if receiving an ambassador in court.

"Marskal, Jepp, and Kral, on an unidentified dragon," I replied, with some bemusement, shaking my head for the absurdity.

"What kind of world are we living in that we even use phrases like 'unidentified dragon,'" she muttered, sliding me a look.

I laughed under my breath, glad to connect with the woman behind the regal mask. "You got here fast," I noted.

"I followed our agreement," she countered.

"The letter of it, anyway." I said it mildly enough. Had she remained in the throne room until I sent word, it would have taken her twice as long to arrive, even at a dead run. I'd timed it.

She elected not to reply, apparently absorbed by the spectacle of Marskal sliding down the dragon's extended leg, followed by Jepp and Kral. My brother wore fighting leathers in the Hawks' style, rather than the Dasnarian armor he'd affected for longer than he'd kept his loyalty to the Empire, though he carried a broadsword as I did. He caught my eye, gestured at the dragon, and shook his head.

I dipped my chin. We lived in interesting times.

Marskal turned to look at the dragon and held out a hand, as if to a lady love, and the immense creature vanished, replaced by Zynda. Clad in a simple, pale-blue silk gown, her long, black hair streaming down her back, the Tala shapeshifter smiled radiantly, and placed her hand on Marskal's arm.

Ursula let out a short breath, too quiet for anyone but me to hear, and too subtle for anyone who didn't know her as well as I did to understand it as sheer vexation. Even knowing shapeshifters could perform such tricks didn't make our minds assimilate such impossible-seeming transitions. Never mind the additional headaches that receiving friendly but gigantic monsters at Ordnung would cause.

With Marskal and Zynda in the lead, Jepp and Kral following behind, the foursome strolled up to us. Arm in arm, they might be honored guests arriving for a ball.

"Your Majesty." Marskal bowed, then saluted in the Hawks' fashion, fist over heart, Jepp echoing the salute. Kral inclined his chin, an expansive gesture of respect for him, while Zynda smiled easily. Extracting her hand from Marskal's arm, she embraced Ursula, kissing her on the cheek.

"It's good to see you, Cousin," she said.

"Likewise," Ursula replied, smiling with warmth, unbending

for the first time in hours. "Though I rather didn't expect to see you on two legs again. Or possibly at all."

Marskal made an odd choking sound and cleared his throat. Zynda shot him an amused look over her shoulder. "Things went better than we hoped," she said, "though it takes a bit of explaining." She arched her finely etched brows in significance, and Ursula took the hint.

"Let's retire to my council chambers," she declared, loudly enough for all to hear. "Court is postponed until afternoon." She caught my pointed glance, but ignored my unspoken opinion that this would be a good opportunity to cancel court entirely for the day. Determined to work herself into the ground.

We passed through the deep outer walls of Ordnung, the gated entrance tunnel casting a deep, cold shadow, a reminder that the warm summer was still tentative and new. There hadn't been enough time for it to fully banish the winter chill. Zynda strolled beside her cousin. Jepp and Marskal, likely out of long habit, marched side by side, conversing quietly, which left my brother and me to bring up the rear.

Hlyti seemed determined today to demonstrate that I couldn't leave the past behind. Though hlyti isn't a deity so much as the force of destiny in Dasnarian thinking, it is capricious, so I sent up a prayer that it would treat us as kindly as possible.

Kral had aged since that last night that all three of us were together. Of course, we'd both aged in the ensuing years. Jenna, however, remained locked in my mind looking as she had that night, forever a girl of eighteen, the last time I laid eyes on her. Unbelievably lovely, even with her ivory hair cropped short—an attempt at disguise—her deep blue eyes enormous in her delicate face, she swam in my clothes. Though four years her junior and nowhere near my adult bulk, I'd already outweighed her by half again as much.

The long sleeves of my shirt at least covered the raw wounds on her wrists and the other injuries she bore on her willowy body. Nothing could hide the haunted look in her eyes.

She'd been happy, though, as much as she could be. We both were, giddy with the prospect of imminent escape, and we'd been ravenous when we'd ordered the meal—food we never ended up eating, because Kral had found us.

I'd learned many lessons that night, all of them deeply painful, and just as deeply embedded.

"You're quiet, rabbit," Kral observed in Dasnarian, and I looked over at him. The age difference between us had vanished over the years. Four years meant little for men our age. Back then, it had meant everything. Though he was a bit younger than Jenna, barely more than a boy himself that night, he'd been far harder than either of us, already chiseled with the cutting edges our parents had carved into him with relentless purpose.

"You're the garrulous one, shark," I replied in the same language. The language of home, bittersweet to me, with its twin threads of cruelty and nostalgia interwoven.

He snorted, eyes lingering on Jepp in front of us. She'd softened him considerably. Immeasurably, really, as I'd never have predicted Kral would turn his back on the ambitions he'd given up his humanity to pursue. He wasn't the same viciously triumphant young man who'd held me at sword point and gloated over his victory.

Nor was I the weaponless fourteen-year-old boy who'd faced the devastating failure to save his sister from her terrible fate. Though Kral and I had made amends when we encountered one another again, it had been more of a tourniquet to stop the mortal blood flow that threatened to taint the present as well as the past. We'd agreed to move forward, as the men we'd become.

But that night hung between us still, hampering easy conversation. I'd think he didn't feel the pain of that unhealed wound as I did, except for the way he searched for things to say to me.

"I've had word from our sister," Kral said, jolting me out of my thoughts. He'd spoken quietly, as if we could be overheard though he still spoke in Dasnarian. All of our companions had picked up varying degrees of our language, so his discretion was well deployed.

Kral's mouth twisted as he gauged the look on my face. "Not *that* sister. Inga."

Ah. "And?" I prompted.

He gestured ahead at Ursula's straight spine. "You'll hear in the debriefing."

"Then why mention it now?"

"Maybe I wanted to see if you'd think I meant Jenna."

Twice in one morning. Hlyti had taken a broadsword to me, done with playing. I said nothing. Could say nothing.

"Silent as a boulder, peaceful as a tree," Kral observed with some cheer, probably pleased at having drawn blood. "The *Skablykrr* does all those dour monks claim, making you silent as the grave that Jenna likely found—"

He didn't complete that foul sentence, breath knocked out of him by the stone wall slamming into his back, his head clapping against it hard enough to daze him. Face pale, icy eyes for once lacking arrogance, he gaped at me over my broadsword laid against his throat.

I could kill him. Silence his mocking superiority for all time.

"Harlan."

Ursula's implacable voice cut through the snarl of my thoughts and jagged emotions. I became aware that Jepp held a dagger to my throat. Marskal on my other side, calming hand on my shoulder. Ursula stepped beside Kral, catching my eye, flicking a warning glance at Jepp, whose dagger point pricked my skin uncomfortably.

"You've gotten faster, brother," Kral wheezed from a tight throat, straining back from my blade, palms raised in surrender.

"Don't speak of her." I said it in Dasnarian, using words of command and warning.

Kral opened his mouth and I sank the blade against his throat, still the flat, but enough of an edge to draw a trickle of blood.

"Harlan," Jepp said evenly. "Don't make me choose between my lover and my queen."

I ignored her. And Ursula, calm and steely as she stared me down.

"Understood?" I asked Kral.

He closed his mouth. Nodded as much as my blade would allow.

I dropped the sword, releasing him, stepped back and sheathed it. Jepp moved immediately to his side, a dagger in each hand, big dark eyes hard on me. She also assessed me with some surprise, a new caution. Finishing the dance, Ursula moved to my side, Marskal still on the other, hand on my shoulder.

"Not speaking of her changes nothing," Kral said to me, still in Dasnarian, rubbing a hand over his throat and inspecting the blood on his fingers. "Some day you're going to have to face the reality that she is—"

I lunged at him, barehanded, but Ursula and Marskal were ready this time. He caught me in a hold—a Dasnarian one I'd taught him, Danu take the man—and though I could've broken it, given a moment more to muster my superior strength, Ursula interposed herself between me and Kral, knowing I'd die before I hurt her.

"What in Danu's freezing tits has gotten into you?" she hissed at me. Beyond her, Jepp kept a wary eye on me, but conferred in furious whispers with Kral.

I took a breath, reaching for the *Skablykrr* calm Kral had mocked. "It's been a thrice-cursed trying day," I muttered at her.

Her expression softened and she laid a hand on my cheek, a rare gesture of public affection. Especially considering that her retinue of guards, along with a good portion of the gate guards, now surrounded us, weapons drawn.

"I apologize," I said to her, and stopped there, hoping she'd understand all the words I couldn't say. Marskal, feeling the killing rage leave my body, relaxed his choke hold and, with another firm and reassuring clasp of my shoulder, stepped back.

"We'll talk later," Ursula promised. She moved back enough to take in both Kral and me at once. "General Kral, please accept the High Throne's apology for violating a truce of hospitality."

Surprised, he looked to her. "Your Majesty." He inclined his head. "No apology needed. I should apologize for baiting my brother. An old argument that elicits… unpredictable reactions."

"Get more predictable, both of you," she replied crisply.

"Yes, your Majesty," I bowed to her, then straightened. Habitually, my hand moved to give her the *Elskastholrr* salute, a promise and reminder, a grounding return to center—and for the first time since I'd made her that promise, I hesitated.

I didn't know if she realized I'd stopped myself, that the conflicts and doubts had seeded themselves in me so deeply that I wasn't sure of myself anymore. She might not have observed it since she'd turned away, dismissing the guards and thanking them for their alert attention. A duty that should've fallen to me, had I not been the cause of it all.

"As we were then," she declared, gesturing Jepp and Kral to

precede us. "Perhaps you should attend to other duties," she said quietly to me. "Burn off some steam."

Marskal lingered close, ready to enforce her commands, no doubt.

"Your Majesty," I said, accepting the implicit judgment. As much as I wanted to affirm—perhaps have her confirm—that my place was at her side, I was in no shape to be in the same room with Kral. "I'll be working out in the training yard if you need me."

I left before she could tell me that she didn't.

$$\sim 7 \sim$$

"Y_OU SHOULD TRY_ playing _I Eat You_," Zynda said, walking beside me. I didn't realize she was there until she'd spoken—a daunting indicator of my level of distraction.

"Shouldn't you be going to the council chambers?" I asked her mildly, to cover the surprise that she'd snuck up on me. Twice in one day, between her and Ursula.

To be fair, the Tala shapeshifters move uncannily fast and silently. Kral was right—I had gotten faster, entirely from sparring with Ursula. Even as a partblood who couldn't actually shapeshift, she could move like lightning striking. Zynda was not only a fullblood, she was likely the most talented shapeshifter alive. It didn't pay to forget that, as much as she seemed to be a graceful and lovely woman in human form, she was also the dragon. Not to mention any number of other lethal and predatory forms I'd seen her take.

She smiled at me, all blue-eyed beauty and friendliness, no frown of concern for my previous behavior. "I will go there. Eventually. But they don't need me for the talk-talk-talking. I loathe that stuff anyway. I'm just the transportation."

I snorted, the half-laugh another surprise. "And I'm just a mercenary soldier."

Her smile took on a rueful twist. "None of our lives are as simple as they once were. But, in fact, Jepp and Kral are the messengers, and Marskal knows everything I do." She shrugged in her languid Tala way, pushing her hair off her shoulders and stretching her arms up to the sun. "Sparring with you gives me an excuse not to have to be inside those horrid stone walls any longer than necessary."

"Are we going to spar?" I asked.

"Yes, thank you!" She smiled radiantly, as if I'd invited her. "When you mentioned the training yard I figured I could be useful, so my cousin won't worry that you're going to kill your brother. Do you want to talk about it?"

"No," I replied definitively.

"Good. I'm a terrible listener." She laughed when I slanted her a glance. "We all have our strengths. If it were me, I'd rather try to kill something than talk about my feelings, too. I'll teach you to play *I Eat You.*"

We'd reached the training yard, now empty with everyone either retired for midday meals or at their guard stations. I'd been planning a good workout, it was true—alone, so I could fume to myself—but sparring with a shapeshifter of Zynda's caliber could be interesting. "All right. What are the rules?"

"Quite simple. I shift to a form, try to best you in it. You counter with something that can top that."

"I can't shapeshift," I pointed out, somewhat unnecessarily.

"But you have many weapons and fighting techniques. Basically, it's a test—which of my forms can best you, which of your weapons can best me. And remember, I heal when I shift, so don't worry about pulling your strikes." She grinned. "Do your worst, mercenary."

"I don't heal magically, so watch your claws, shapeshifter." This began to sound fun. With my blood still hot, I drew my sword, swinging it to loosen my muscles.

Her smile took on a feral edge. "Just try not to actually kill me. Marskal would be most put out and we don't need any more manly displays today." With that taunt, she shifted into a tiger. I barely registered the sight of the big cat—astonishingly orange, ribbed in black warning stripes, mouth opened in a mighty snarl that had frozen plenty of warriors in their shoes—before she leapt at me.

I barely dodged those lethal claws, coming up under her belly with an upward, two-handed heave of the broadsword that connected with a satisfying bite. Or started to, because she vaporized at the edge of my blade, becoming a raptor that dove with a shriek. Talons slashed down my upraised arm before I countered with a hastily drawn short blade, my broadsword heavy in one hand on a backstroke too distant to bring it to bear in time.

Next time, I'd make a pile of weapons to access. A bow or spear would be handy. The raptor—was it an eagle? I couldn't get a clear look at her and it didn't matter—buffeted me with stunning blows of its wings, hooked beak going for my eyes. I dropped the sword, as it was too big for close infighting like this, and seized the bird by the slender neck, squeezing.

And found myself embracing a fucking grizzly bear. My fisted hand slid uselessly off the thick throat as the bear roared in my face, stopping my heart, and then wrapped its great arms around me in a deadly vise so that my spine cracked, the fanged jaws closing over my head. I was done for. I'd be so done for if this was to the death.

But I still had my dagger and I drove it up, into the soft cavity under the rib cage, into its heart, putting all of my muscle into it. Hot blood gushed over my hand, along with entrails and the scrape of bone resisting, then cracking. I roared, too, into the bear's steaming maw, my defiance and rage in the face of death.

And it was gone.

Zynda—remarkably composed in her pretty blue dress, hair sleek and flowing—stood barefoot before me with a slender hand pressed over her heart. Her eyes huge and dark blue as the deepest ocean regarded me with shock. "Moranu, Harlan—I told you not to kill me!"

I looked down at my dagger hand, covered in blood and gore. Why did the fleshly aspects of the bear remain when the animal itself had vanished? In this, too, I shared Ursula's uneasiness with shapeshifting. A profoundly strange magic. "You had my entire head in your jaws," I pointed out, very reasonably. "All you had to do was bite down a fraction more to end me."

"Yes, but I didn't," she snapped. Then burst out laughing. "Well played, Dasnarian. I'm only glad Zyr didn't see this. He'd never let me hear the end of it. Beaten by a mossback."

I found myself grinning back at her and rolled my head on my neck, feeling the bear's bruising grip in my spine. "My ancestors thank you. I'm sure more than one faced an actual grizzly in the forests of Dasnaria."

"Two out of three?" she suggested with raised brows.

It had felt good not to have to hold back. "You're on. But I'm stockpiling some weapons for this round."

"Sure." She pretended to examine her nails like a lady of court. "But I won't go so easy on you this time."

"Same," I told her.

"When I suggested you burn off some steam, I didn't mean get yourself killed," Ursula said with considerable asperity as she walked into her chambers.

She would've been informed that I'd requested a Tala healer to attend my worst wounds, so it didn't surprise me that she already knew. Just as well that I'd gone to her rooms and not elsewhere. I'd considered it, whether I'd be welcome in the chambers that had been hers long before her father hired my Vervaldr to defend Ordnung. Ursula referred to them as our rooms, but I was careful not to. Finally I'd decided that she'd tell me in no uncertain terms when she wanted me out.

She'd left the decision in my lap, so I'd keep that tactical advantage.

"I didn't get myself killed," I replied mildly. "As you, with your acute observational skills, can no doubt confirm for yourself."

"How is he?" she asked the Tala healer, Kelleah, ignoring me entirely.

"A few broken ribs, a lot of lacerations, some internal bleeding. Nothing I can't fix, given a few more moments of quiet," Kelleah replied, voice vague and green eyes sharp. A wide-shouldered and big-bosomed woman with an unusual amount of red in her Tala dark hair, Kelleah possessed both the gentle, nurturing qualities of a healer and the no-nonsense conviction of those who put their calling above all else. Andi had sent her to be Ordnung's healer, remarking that Kelleah would be up to the challenge of defying Ursula when necessary.

Duly rebuked, clearly not happy about it, Ursula divested herself of the trappings of her public persona. First she tossed the crown aside, then removed her jewelry, treating her mother's rubies with a reverence she hadn't shown the crown. She unbuckled her sword belt from the metalwork bodice and set the whole thing—sword still sheathed—on the table. One of her ladies approached at her glance and undid the fastenings of the bodice, taking it away.

Apparently Ursula planned to stay in for a bit. I couldn't decide if that boded well or ill for me. At least she was unarmed. With external weapons, anyway.

She stretched—nothing like Zynda's languid movements, but like a warrior relieved of armor—and prowled to the window behind me. Her soft bootsteps on the thick rugs continued, and I pictured her pacing restlessly. Kelleah's healing magic swarmed through me, an odd prickling heat that made me profoundly sleepy and restless at once. I resisted the sleepiness, focusing on the surging energy. I'd need it for whatever confrontation Ursula planned—almost certainly not of the enticing variety. Alas.

Tala healing—we all knew from experience—tended to arouse sexual desire along with the renewed wellbeing. The more intense the healing, the more extreme the ensuing arousal. Except when the patient nearly died, as Ursula had. Then it was all they could do to muster the will to live. Aha—and that memory worked to dampen any ill-considered desire on my part.

I sincerely doubted Ursula would appreciate any seductive moves from the man she thought had betrayed her and had lost his temper, shaming her royal hospitality.

"There," Kelleah declared, rubbing her palms together briskly, the green of her eyes dimming as she allowed the healing magic to settle inside her again. "You'll be just fine, Captain Harlan." Her gaze darted to Ursula, still standing rigidly by the window. "At least physically." She winked encouragingly and stood. "Your Majesty," she said, by way of signaling her withdrawal, and strode out.

Servants passed her, bringing in platters of food and wine, then also left, closing the doors and leaving us alone.

"Didn't you eat yet?" I asked Ursula, surveying the spread,

and the midafternoon sun.

"Yes. And no." She sounded distracted, deep in thought, but came over to sit opposite me. With her crown removed, she'd been running her hands through her bloodred hair so it stood in unruly tufts and spikes. Endearingly so. Her composed expression and shuttered gaze didn't show it, but the mussed hair gave evidence of her agitation.

I reached over the table and took her hand, so wiry and strong, callused from wielding her sword. "I'm sorry if I worried you. My wounds weren't that severe. Under other circumstances, I'd have dealt with them on my own. I only asked for Kelleah in case there's an attack. I need to be in top form."

She squeezed my hand, meeting my eyes—hers indeed filled with worry. "It's not that," she said, then amended, withdrawing her hand. "Well, hearing that Zynda had torn you up enough that you called for Kelleah didn't help my appetite. But, no, I had no stomach to eat with the others, and I knew you hadn't eaten. Due to the aforementioned and ill-advised battle to the death with the best shapeshifter living."

"It wasn't a battle to the death," I corrected, filling my plate. Magical healing left you hungry, too. "We only sparred."

"Sparred," she echoed, the neutrality of her tone an accusation in and of itself.

I quickly checked her expression, but it revealed nothing. "Yes. A game, nothing more."

"Oh, it was more than that. It was foolish and irresponsible," she bit out "Either of you could've killed the other and we need you both in the war ahead. One slip, Harlan, that's all it takes. One wound mortal enough that she can't shift in time or the Tala healer can't reach you. For a *game*. She wasn't supposed to be out there with you anyway. *Sparring*."

I watched her closely as she finished by spitting the word

through tight lips. We *had* been foolish and irresponsible, Zynda and I. She'd beaten me two rounds out of three—the third time only because she pulled out the dragon form—and I'd been the one to insist on a fourth, with the dragon off the table as the worst kind of cheating. That last match had indeed nearly killed us, both of us carried away in our determination to best the other. We'd finally conceded to the tie and she'd had to lend a shoulder to help me stagger back into the castle.

Ursula, however, was more than worried, more than aggravated with me. Something had her in a quiet fury, something newer than this morning's trials.

Ursula and I usually sparred together, and it often led to sex. It hadn't occurred to me that she might see my sparring with Zynda as another betrayal. "Are you jealous?"

"No, I'm not *jealous*," she sneered, lathering a slice of rye bread with fresh butter. Then she sighed, closing her eyes briefly. "All right, maybe a little jealous."

"Essla…" I wished I still had ahold of her. "I'm in no way attracted to Zynda. You are the only woman I want. Ever. You're everything to me."

She met my gaze wryly. "So you're forever telling me. And it's not that. I'm more…bothered that you sparred with her instead of talking to me about what's going on." She held up the honey-stick, the thick liquid forming golden teardrops, pointing it at me to forestall any explanation. "I'm also envious that you two got to be outside, playing games, while I was stuck in the council chambers talking obnoxious politics."

I chewed thoughtfully. The butter tasted of sweet clover, redolent of summer, and the warm afternoon sunshine brought in the sounds of furious birdsong and the faint echoes of music and laughter. Ursula didn't have Andi's same drive to be outdoors, to live outside of walls, which seemed to be characteristic of the Tala, but she had enough Tala in her to feel the pull. When she'd been her father's heir, Ursula had traveled extensively through the realm, leading campaigns or exercising Uorsin's diplomatic overtures. On our travels, we'd been outside more than in.

Since returning to Ordnung and taking up the weight of her crown again, it had been the reverse. She'd barely been able to enjoy the summer weather at all. No wonder she acted so caged lately. Maybe I could do something about that.

Though not today.

"I take it the politics were obnoxious enough for you to cancel court for the afternoon?" I asked carefully.

"As obnoxious as they get," she agreed, then poured us both wine, filling the goblets to the rim. An ominous sign for so early in the day. "You and I need to talk."

~ 8 ~

H AD THERE EVER been another phrase to strike such terror in a man's heart? I could've wished to be more clear headed, free of the dregs of the healing magic, but I'd brought this on myself and I'd withstand the storm.

"All right," I said, helping myself to more food, acting as calm as possible. "You know I always enjoy conversing with you."

She slammed her palms on the table, jolting the dishes and destabilizing the wine pitcher. I caught it before it toppled, setting it back carefully and eyeing her. "Stop managing me," she ground out. The measured words might as well have been shouted.

I put down my food and rubbed my palms on thighs. "I'm not managing you. I'm doing my best to keep this conversation calm and reasonable."

"Oh, is that so?" Her eyebrows climbed along with her tone. "You mean, calm and reasonable like when you attacked Kral?"

Setting my teeth, but keeping my jaw relaxed so she wouldn't read that tic of mine, one she knew well, I picked up a fresh slice of bread and began to meticulously coat it with an even film of butter. Witness my manful control. "I apologize for that lapse. He goaded me in exactly the way he knew how to get to me."

"Then it had to do with Jenna."

Three times. Jenna's name spoken aloud for the third time in one day.

Though I'd thought I'd left Dasnarian superstitions behind, I reflexively scanned the room, half expecting her ghost to appear, summoned by the incautious incantation. Would she rail at me? Weep, perhaps, and rightfully accuse me of having been too weak and stupid to save her?

The butter tasted sour now, the fresh-baked bread like ash. I set it aside and scrubbed my hands over my face. "Yes," I replied. "It had to do with her."

Ursula sat back in her chair, angling it so she could extend her long legs, crossing them at her booted ankles. "You once told me that old pains fester like unhealed wounds, that we think they've healed, but they've only scabbed over, with the pus growing in the dark. Until something happens to break them open."

I eyed her. "There are few blows that sting more than having one's own words flung back in one's face."

She smiled slightly, more a grimace of sympathy. "I know that well, as you do it to me all the time."

I laughed a little, dry and without humor.

"That was a lot of pus I saw today," she said.

I gazed back at her, and she refilled my wine cup, which I'd already emptied. Another bad sign. "Is this what you wanted to talk about—or is it whatever news Jepp and Kral brought?"

"Both, actually." She had unhappy lines around her mouth. "They are ... intertwined."

I nodded, not understanding, but wondering. Kral needling me about Jenna after all this time hadn't been a coincidence. In my experience, very little in life is a coincidence. I blame hlyti.

"I did cancel court this afternoon," Ursula continued, "so you and I can sort all of this out. I can't... I need to lock this part of my life down before I can deal with anything else."

A profound failure on my part, a failure to the *Elskastholrr* that I caused her difficulty instead of being a solid foundation. "Which first, then—yours or mine?"

She regarded me calmly. "I'm sorry to force you into this, so your choice."

Time to clean up my own mess, then we'd see if we had anything left in us to address whatever news Kral had brought that was dire enough for Ursula to cancel court.

"I was fourteen years old," I told her, "and the youngest of my siblings."

As I spoke, it seemed the formal chill of the Imperial Palace settled around us. The opulent carpets that muffled the boot-steps of the men and silenced the barefoot tread of the elegant women. The scent of jasmine and the delicate chime of jewelry as they drifted past, wreathed in colorful silk, gazes demurely averted. Mysterious and enticing.

"Six brothers," Ursula prompted, bringing me out of the reverie.

"Yes, and three sisters. All of us born in four years to three wives."

"Your father was a busy man—and his wives hard-worked."

"Yes." I splayed my hands on the table, so like my father's. Big and blunt. The hands of a warrior, not a statesman. The hands of a brutally cruel and domineering man. "He became emperor later than he wished—having spent many years in various wars, adding to the empire for his father—and set to making heirs with due diligence."

I lifted my gaze to hers, and raised a brow. "In Dasnaria, the emperor is not only divine, but expected to demonstrate his manly virility by producing as many children by as many women as possible."

"Of course," she replied softly, eyes a softer gray now with sympathy at whatever she saw in mine.

"Of course," I echoed, wryly. "So, that number doesn't include the multitudes of illegitimate half-siblings I have. I have no idea how many. Of the ten legitimate children born to his three wives, we are in order of birth: my eldest sister—whose name I've vowed never to speak aloud, but that you know—then Hestar, Kral, Inga, Ban, Helva, Mykal, Leo, Loke, and myself."

"So many," she murmured and picked up her wine, though she didn't drink. "And which are your full siblings?"

"Hestar—now emperor—Helva, Leo and Loke. Those last two are identical twins." I smiled despite my grim mood, remembering the trouble the golden twins of mischief had gotten into.

"You're full brother to the Emperor of Dasnaria," she mused, looking into her wine. "Does that mean anything significant?"

"It doesn't change anything materially, no. For the most part, birth order decides the hierarchy, though the status of the mother does, too. My mother was second wife."

"Was?"

"Died long ago." I met Ursula's intent gaze evenly. "My mother was named Jilliya. She was never in good health, not as long as I can remember."

"She bore five children in four years. Even with two of them twins, that would be enough to ruin the health of any woman," Ursula pointed out.

"True. And Hulda, first wife, had a deft hand with poison."

Ursula's mouth parted slightly, but she took that in, drinking a good draught of her wine. She drank less now than when I met her, which I liked to think I'd influenced, if only by helping her find other ways to unwind enough to sleep. I didn't begrudge her the choice this afternoon. Didn't begrudge either of us.

"So much you've never told me," she commented.

I laced my fingers together into one fist, steadying it on the table. "I'm sorry for that. I'm telling you now. Everything I can speak aloud. Whatever you want to know."

"All right." She inclined her head. "So Jenna was your half-sister and—does it hurt you for me to speak her name? You flinched just then."

I blew out a breath, aware it came out shaky. "No. It's… just shocking. To hear it. So is the past tense."

"I apologize. That was thoughtless of me. She *is* your half-sister."

"Yes. My half-sister. Kral's full sister, both of them born to Hulda. And past tense is likely accurate. She almost certainly died two decades ago. It's a… reality I've never quite grappled with." A headache throbbed behind my eyes and I squeezed the bridge of my nose between thumb and knuckled forefinger, aware of the moisture there. Soon I'd be sobbing like a toddler.

"Harlan." Ursula sounded broken, as she so rarely did. She stood beside me and her hand covered mine. I opened my arms to her and she slipped onto my lap, all delicate bones and yielding softness. She leaned into me and I buried my face against her silky hair that looked like blood and fire, but tasted of grace. "You're the one who's good at this," she finally said. "Do you want to stop or keep going?"

"The wound is open," I replied with grim determination, "so let's continue purging the pus."

"All right then. So, as eldest child born to the first wife, Jenna would've been heir, had she been a boy."

I smiled, brushing my lips against her forehead. The sharpest of minds—and practiced at keeping track of royal politics, much as she groused about it. "Correct. So Hestar was heir, with Kral in second place—though a close one, with his mother being the Empress. I didn't understand much of this back then. I was a boy, the baby, and I was entirely caught up in training to fight well enough that my brothers couldn't beat me into letting them run my life—and with the enticing prospect of bedding my first woman on my upcoming birthday."

She laughed, sweet against me. "I can only imagine your devotion to that particular threshold."

"Yes." I tipped her chin up and kissed her, needing it. To my great relief, she returned the kiss, opening her mouth to me and winding her long arms around my neck. I sank into her, savoring her intensity and passion. So rarely did I have her undivided attention. She smiled at me, caressing my cheek with her rough fingers, all womanly softness for the moment, all mine. For the moment.

"I was a callow youth," I continued, thinking back to my past self. "Self-absorbed as adolescents are, terribly spoiled as the baby of the family. When it came time for my eldest sister to be married, I was filled with excitement. There would be parties and I would get to see her, Inga, and Helva again for the first time in seven years."

"Why so long?" Ursula interrupted with a frown. "Didn't you all live in the Imperial Palace?"

"Yes, but the Imperial Princesses all remained in the seraglio. I spent my early years in there with them, the other wives and ladies, and my mother. Around age seven, though, the boys leave the seraglio to begin to learn to be men, and the girls stay behind." I smoothed the line between her brows with my thumb. "It's a strange practice, I know—and one I can't abide now—but back then I was actually jealous of my sisters that they got to stay. The seraglio of the Imperial Palace is still one of the most beautiful places I've ever seen. An enclosed world, lush and tropical, with lagoons and palm trees. We played all day and were indulged in every way. Leaving it… well, that was a cold awakening to what felt like a much harsher world. I would cry myself to sleep at night—silently, so my brothers wouldn't hear and use it against me—missing my mother and my sisters. I felt sorry for myself." I laughed, a bitter edge to it, for my selfishness.

"Of course you grieved," Ursula replied, still frowning. "Ripping a child that age from everything he's known would be terribly traumatic."

"And yet, I was a privileged idiot because I didn't understand that I was the lucky one. I still had no idea when seven years later my eldest sister turned eighteen and her marriage was arranged to one of our father's favored subject kings, Rodolf of Arynherk. I was more excited for that wedding—for all my siblings to be together—than I'd been for anything in my life." The jubilation of my younger self shamed me now. "Until I began to listen to the talk in the training yard, the way the other men snickered about Rodolf, speculating about what he'd done to his other wives, four of them, all dead young. They called him Bloody Rodolf, and the things they said about him, dark things, sexual things…" I had to stop, unable to say them aloud, especially not to Ursula, who'd suffered at the hands of a monster, too.

But she lay soft against me still, calm and understanding. "For a boy who had yet to lie with a woman that had to be shocking to hear."

"Yes." I wrapped my arms around her, as if I could protect her from her past, protect Jenna from the terrible things I had been powerless to prevent. "I'd had a boy's ideals about women and sex, that it would be all about soft skin and perfume and gentle delights."

"Like the seraglio had been in your childhood," she murmured.

"Ah." That hadn't occurred to me. "I suppose so." I tucked that idea away to examine later. "So when Inga and my eldest sister emerged from the seraglio for the first time in their lives… I learned so much that night."

About beauty and power.

And betrayal.

~ 9 ~

"They were both astonishingly beautiful," I remembered. "As elegant and polished as the wealth of an empire could create. My eldest sister had inherited her mother's beauty—and Empress Hulda was famous for her ivory hair and extraordinary deep blue eyes. On top of that, my eldest sister had lived all her life indoors, with only magical light, away from the sun, so her skin was fair and unblemished, her hair only shades darker. And they'd dressed her in white silk, diamonds and pearls. She took my breath away." I frowned. "I don't mean that to sound..."

"It doesn't," Ursula murmured. "She was dazzling. Your beloved sister and the epitome of feminine beauty. You probably worshipped her."

"I did, yes." I rubbed my hand along her back, grateful she understood. "I was in awe of her and I wanted to save her. I warned her about Rodolf, told her she should break off the engagement. But she wouldn't listen. I figured it was because I was only a boy and not worth paying attention to.

"She married him, and they stayed in the Imperial Palace for a week. She was always either with *him*"—my voice shook, and I had to steady it—"or in the seraglio where I couldn't go. Everyone was so happy, celebrating the royal wedding. When I asked about her, everyone told me not to worry, that she was

63

fine.

"But we had a reception for her that last night before she left on her wedding journey to travel with him to his kingdom—a party for her that she actually got to attend—a *party*. And, oh, Essla…" I had to pause to catch my breath. "She was so changed. He'd broken her. They'd covered her pretty skin with makeup, but I could see the bruises beneath. And her klút—her gown—covered more of her, and they'd given her gloves to wear under her wedding bracelets, but I could tell by the way she flinched, how she hunched into herself that the cur had hurt her in terrible ways."

Ursula made a sound, and I stopped, fully aware of the parallels, how Ursula had submitted to whatever her own father expected of her. "Is this too difficult for you to hear, given what Uorsin did to you?"

"It's not easy," she admitted, still not looking at me. "I want to say I'm over that and it's in the past, but we both know that would be a lie. And what happened to me was nothing like this. I want you to keep going. I begin to understand, though, how you could see so much in me, so easily."

Not easily. Nothing about Ursula had been easy. I squeezed her reassuringly, then relaxed my hold. "I asked her if he'd hit her and she *laughed*. Laughed in my face, and I realized that what she'd been through was so much worse than that. I wanted her to appeal to our father, her mother, to Hestar, heir apparent. I begged her to tell them, to show them her injuries."

"She told you they knew and it wouldn't matter anyway," Ursula guessed.

"How did you know?"

She shrugged a little, her cheek against my chest. "You were a sexually innocent boy of fourteen. If you could see it, imagine how much better the adults could recognize the signs. If you'd heard the gossip, then everyone knew about Bloody Rodolf. Jenna probably understood far better than you did how little recourse she had."

"What you and my sister saw so clearly came as an astonishing blow to me. I spoke to our father, to Hestar, to Kral, and my other brothers about the situation and… they didn't care. She was an Imperial Princess and must do her duty to the family and the empire. We all served the Konyngrr fist; a woman's lot fell to her. She accepted it—why couldn't I?"

"Because you've never had it in you to accept injustice of any kind," Ursula replied. "One of the many things I love about you."

I breathed in her scent and the reassurance that she could still speak so easily of loving me. So surreal to be telling this story after all the years of silence, but I couldn't imagine anyone else I'd rather tell. Could have told, for that matter. "My sister—she told me to forget her. And she said…" The anguish knotted my throat. "She told me goodbye, and said that if I want to do something for her, to treat the women in my life well in her memory."

"And you have," Ursula said softly. She must have been weeping because my shirt had gone damp under her cheek. "You are the best of men, Harlan. She'd be so proud."

I kissed her forehead, beyond grateful for those words. "But the story doesn't end there."

"Of course not," she said, her voice dry now. "Because you're you."

I chuckled, relieved to feel my chest relax. "Well, and I was an impetuous young man with more ideals than sense. But I also was an Imperial Prince, and I used that status to bully the Arynherk guards into allowing me to join their entourage. I stayed out of Rodolf's sight, not that he'd pay much attention to a minor princeling like me, and kept to the middle-ranking officers—intimidating them with liberal use of my father's name and probable wrath, avoiding anyone with enough rank to know I shouldn't be there."

"Nicely played." Ursula's admiration did excellent things for my ego, even for something I'd done long ago.

"I'm surprised in retrospect that I pulled it off."

"Youthful bravado goes a long way."

"Very true. My sister, when she saw I'd come along, very nearly gave it all away in her panic. She wanted to protect *me*, begged me to go back before I was found out."

"I can understand that," Ursula commented.

Of course she would, being the eldest sister, always taking care of the others. "But my mind was made up and I refused."

"Stubborn, even then."

I let that go as true enough. "The farther we traveled from the Imperial Palace, the laxer the seraglio rules were in the noble households where Rodolf planned to overnight. In the smaller manors and keeps, it's simply not practical or healthy for the women to live in a closed set of rooms all day, every day. That openness would work in our favor. I also knew once we reached Arynherk, I'd be dealing with people loyal to Rodolf, so if I was going to help my sister escape, then it had to be before then."

Ursula sat up and looked at me. "You helped her to escape?"

"Of course." I frowned, puzzled. "That was my plan all along."

"Oh, thank Danu," she breathed and framed my face with her warrior's hands, kissing me deeply. "I can't stand suspense. Tell me she escaped with you."

"She escaped with me."

Ursula let out a long breath. "Unreal. You are a remarkable man."

I smoothed a wayward lock of her hair back from her temple. "Thank you, but I was mostly insanely lucky. When I look back at all the ways my plan could've failed..." I shook off the specter of those nightmare scenarios, some that still visited me in harrowing dreams.

"I broke her out in the middle of the night and we traveled through... a cold climate." I hedged my way judiciously through the details I'd sworn not to reveal. "And made for a... place where we could travel out of the empire."

Ursula settled back against me. "This is like a riddle. I'm guessing you went through remote countryside, probably crossing mountains if it was so much colder, to a coastal city where you could sail elsewhere. Smart plan."

"Not so much. As with all plans, but especially those contrived by inexperienced fools, it went awry." I sighed heavily. "I need to move."

She obligingly stood, uncoiling herself with grace and a hint of the speed from her shapeshifter heritage. Taking the opportunity, she refilled our wine goblets and met me by the window with them. Handing me mine, she touched hers to it in grave salute. "To an idealistic boy who did what no one else had the courage to attempt."

I smiled slightly, mostly to please her, and sipped, steeling myself for the next part. "We couldn't travel as swiftly as I'd assumed. My experience had been with other men, ones properly dressed for bitter weather and skilled at riding. My sister... she had never even sat a horse before. Though I'd found outdoor gear for her, it had all been designed for men." I swallowed some wine, grateful for the way it blurred the sharp edges of those desperate memories.

"And she'd been hurt," Ursula supplied, gaze full of sorrow.

"Yes. The women... they used teas and a soothing smoke to

ease pain. Another aspect of life in the Imperial Palace I'd been aware of but never thought through." I lifted my wine in grim acceptance. "My sister had been drugged into a stupor and I made her give up the smoke and tea so she'd be alert for the escape."

"You had to." Ursula nodded crisply. "No choice there. And she did it, which speaks to her strength of character."

If only I'd known someone like Ursula then. I could've used her clear thinking. "She was so brave, Essla. She never once complained, but she was in terrible pain, injured far worse than I knew, where no one could see."

Ursula nodded, understanding, the ghost of old pain tightening her face. I nearly asked again if I should stop, remembering what she'd told me about herself, how she'd been so young, and she'd bled, telling no one. She wouldn't thank me, though, for treating her as too fragile to hear this.

"I didn't know until we reached the hunter's cabin I'd been making for. We'd made it away clean and rode through the night, but morning would bring discovery of her absence and inevitable pursuit. I'd hoped to rest a few hours, then continue. But her saddle blankets…" I rubbed a hand over my face, wiping away the cold sweat. "Soaked in blood."

"Not surprising, really," Ursula said the words very softly, laying a hand on my arm and stroking me. "A young and virgin bride and a man of Bloody Rodolf's reputation…"

"Yes, well." I wrapped my hands around the goblet, holding onto it. "I didn't know that. I wasn't even entirely clear on how women differed from men, other than ribald jokes and improbable tales. But I had to do *something*. She was so pale and weak— even I could see she'd die if we kept going that way."

"What did you do?" Ursula asked, the knowing in her eyes.

"She was ashamed, embarrassed, didn't want me to know

and certainly didn't want her baby brother seeing her that way." It had been so surreal, her embarrassment and mine, along with the keen awareness that her life, at the least, rode on both of us setting those niceties aside. My lovely sister, and the savagery of what he'd done to her tenderest, most intimate self.

"He'd torn her badly, in her sex, so I sewed her up. I knew enough of field dressing wounds, how to clean them, of stitches and so forth. What I didn't know was…" I gave Ursula a look I hoped was wry, though it felt like it fell short. She only watched me with solemn attention. "I didn't know what a healthy woman's sex should look like," I explained. "I didn't know what was a natural opening and what—" My voice broke.

Ursula took my goblet, set it aside, and drew me into her arms; so much slighter than I, but strong enough to hold me as I dropped my forehead to her shoulder. "Oh, Harlan," she murmured. "You are an incredible man, then and now. And she lived. That's what matters."

"She lived. And I made myself some promises that night."

"You swore to learn your way around women so well that you would know what to do both to give them pleasure and to heal?" Ursula suggested, a wry knowing in her voice.

I lifted my head and kissed her forehead. "Yes."

"I can vouch for your success." She kissed me, a tender brush of her lips against mine, gentle in a way she rarely was. "What then?"

"We were extraordinarily lucky—or so I believed—and though we stayed in that cabin for days, long enough for her to heal sufficiently to at least ride, we weren't discovered. We made it to my planned destination, and I paid for passage on transportation to leave in the morning. My sister had shorn her distinctive hair and we'd found a sympathetic blacksmith to cut off her wedding bracelets, and unchain her ring. We'd—"

Ursula held up her index finger, stopping me. She'd broken that finger a few times in sword practice or battles, and it had a crooked bent, as if it asked a question. "Cut off her bracelets, and… unchain a ring?" she inquired, a hint of danger beneath the smooth surface tone.

I sighed. She was going to hate this. "Dasnarian wedding bracelets are an old tradition. They're jeweled and very pretty—all different designs—but traditionally they're locked onto the bride during the wedding ceremony, never to be removed." More like manacles than jewelry, it had occurred to me much later in life.

Ursula assimilated that with a cool and remote expression, saying nothing.

"The ring… Well, Bloody Rodolf had this extraordinary diamond ring, an Arynherk tradition, that he gave my sister to go with the bracelets—and attached to them by a chain. They all had to be cut off and the jewels were going to pay for our new lives."

"'Our'?" She still sounded distant, mastering her revulsion, I knew.

"I planned to go with her. My sister… she knew nothing of the world. She'd been raised very deliberately that way. I'd never thought about it—as I'd never thought about so many things back then, in my selfishness—but she'd been educated only in pleasing her husband. You know already that Dasnarian women can't handle money or make trade transactions of any kind, by law of the empire, but my sister couldn't even count."

"Of course you had to go with her." Ursula picked up her wine again and sipped, considering me, her thoughts obscure.

"And I had no wish to return to my life," I admitted. "I couldn't be a part of a family who did that to their own. I wanted nothing more of being an Imperial Prince and all that entailed."

"Which is why you were so angry with me the day Kral arrived at Ordnung, and I called you Prince Harlan Konyngrr," she noted.

"Yes." I grimaced, acknowledging. "You understand more now why I am not… entirely rational on the topic."

"I do." She gazed out the window at the lovely summer afternoon, her profile sharp, her bearing so regal. "I won't beat you up about this, but you could have explained. It would've helped to know before now."

I brushed a hand over her hair, less an apology than an effort to demonstrate what I had no words to express. She gave me a sidelong look, and shook her head. "Finish it. What happened?"

"Kral found us."

"Kral." She pressed her lips together. "I see."

"He tracked us. Caught me naked in the bath, my weapons on the other side of the room."

She winced in sympathy and I knew she, of all people, would understand that level of nakedness, of powerlessness.

"He intended to escort us back to face our father, said all would be forgiven if we gave him no trouble. My sister, of course, would be returned to her husband, who owned her under Dasnarian law."

Ursula set down her goblet and leaned against the window sill, breathing the fresh air, her knuckles white. "I'm sorry I stopped you from killing him," she said conversationally.

"No, it's good you stopped me."

"Oh, right." She gave me a lethal smile. "Because now we can go kill him together."

~ 10 ~

S HE MEANT IT, too, gray eyes sharp as a silver blade. No matter that Ursula claimed the priorities of the High Throne overrode all else, where she loved, she loved fiercely and without reservation. And as Danu's avatar, she couldn't abide injustice, especially wrongs against other women. I laughed, running a hand down her back, more in love with this warrior of a woman than ever.

"Jepp would never forgive us," I pointed out.

"Jepp," she said reflectively. "How she can love a man like that?"

"Because he's changed." I held up my hands when her gaze narrowed and sparked. "He has. You have to realize he was only a youth, too. At seventeen, he had years of bulk and fighting skill on me, but he was, if anything, more selfish, more narrow-minded, able to see only one path, one ambition."

She snorted, but didn't interrupt.

"He believed that he'd be made heir in Hestar's place, as a reward for bringing us back."

"Would your father have done that?"

I lifted a shoulder and let it fall. "Who knows? Kral believed he would, and his mother Hulda molded him to want nothing but that, except perhaps her approval—which, along with her love, hinged entirely on Kral ascending to the throne instead of

Hestar. Kral…didn't have it in him to have compassion for our sister. None of us were raised to have compassion for the weak, or for the women we believed existed to slake our needs and nothing else."

She contemplated that—and me. "However did you emerge from that as the man you are now?"

I refilled my goblet and hers. "I broke into pieces and put myself back together in another pattern."

"I see. So, Kral had you trapped and captive…?"

"Kral underestimated her. It never occurred to him that she'd act without my help, so he left her for the night in her own room at the inn and made me sleep in his." I raised my brows. "Anything else wouldn't have been proper."

"She escaped in the night?" Ursula breathed, a hint of delight in it.

"She did." I couldn't help smiling also. "She must've climbed out the windows and made her way over the rooftops. No one saw or heard a thing. She was a dancer, did I mention that? I saw her dance the ducerse the night before her wedding, and she was stunning. You would appreciate the athletic skill of it. She wore bells, but danced so that they remained silent until she allowed them to chime." I shook my head, remembering Jenna, her ivory hair like a banner of silk, gleaming with pearls and sparkling with diamonds, dancing as I'd never seen anyone dance, before or since.

"In the morning she was gone, leaving only that diamond ring behind. She arranged it just so, in the carcass of the fowl Kral had eaten for dinner. You should've seen Kral's face." I laughed, and Ursula laughed with me, the light of vengeance bright in her eyes.

"Good girl," she murmured. "Good for you." Her expression sharpened. "Surely Kral searched for her."

"Of course—and dragged me with him, also of course. She wasn't on the transportation I'd booked. No one had seen her."

Ursula looked interested, loving the puzzle. "She left the diamond but had the other jewels, and you have to be talking sailing ships. So, she set sail for somewhere else."

I lifted one shoulder and let it fall. "Or she was enslaved."

Ursula frowned, shocked out of her reverie. "Excuse me?"

"You, yourself, accused me of being from a race of slavers when we first met," I pointed out. "While not entirely accurate, it's also not entirely untrue. My sister was a lovely, nubile young woman, clearly of gentle birth, with no protection, no way to defend herself beyond a few last-resort moves I showed her with a dagger."

Ursula smiled briefly. "Of course you did. But she might've found friends. There are good people in the world, too."

I touched her cheek. "You are the idealist, though you try to act so tough."

She narrowed her eyes in menace. "I *am* tough."

"You are," I conceded. "My sister… was not." I could only wish she'd been trained as Ursula had, to be a warrior, to survive.

"I don't know, Harlan." Ursula thoughtfully turned the goblet in her hands. "The woman you describe is no fragile flower. She gutted it out on that ride, gave up the drugs when she had to be in horrendous pain—climbed out a window and disappeared. She sounds like a survivor to me."

"Then why didn't I find her? Why didn't she find me?" I tossed back the rest of my wine, the grit in the dregs of it scraping my throat.

"I take it you looked."

"Later, yes. After I left the third time."

"The third?"

"Yes. So, once Kral—to his intense fury and frustration, which I greatly enjoyed—couldn't find any trace of our sister, we journeyed back to the Imperial Palace. No surprise, though I went peaceably enough, all was not forgiven." I smiled without humor as Ursula's gaze darkened. "My father, the emperor; Empress Hulda; my brother Hestar; Kral—they all brought considerable pressure on me to reveal where my sister had gone."

"You didn't tell them you didn't know?"

"Sure I did. They didn't believe me. If I hadn't helped her final escape, then they'd have to accept that a young woman, barely more than a girl, whom they'd devoted enormous effort into molding to be obedient and helpless, had somehow succeeded at defying them all. Which is more likely?"

She nodded, slowly, then looked at me with concern. "What pressure did they put on you?"

I lifted a shoulder and let it fall. "It was long ago, and the young man I was no longer needs defending."

"I'll decide what needs defending. What pressure?"

"The usual, Essla," I told her wearily. "What you'd imagine—beatings, flogging, starvation, back-breaking work, humiliating me by stripping me of rank, of what little power I possessed."

"I'm so sorry, Harlan," she murmured, looking bereft.

"As I said, it was long ago, and it did a great deal to strengthen me. I learned a lot about myself and what I could withstand. I discovered they couldn't do anything to me that I wouldn't willingly suffer, as I always had in my mind's eye how much worse my sister had suffered, simply for existing. Eventually, however, they discovered something I couldn't bear."

"Your mother, and your other sisters," Ursula guessed, then smiled ruefully at what she saw in my face. "Standard technique for breaking someone, yes? If you can't break them, hurt someone else in their stead. I bet it worked, too."

"It did. You know, through all that, I still hadn't seen Helva. She was only fifteen and not old enough to leave the seraglio and attend the wedding *festivities*. But they brought her out to be flogged. Her and Inga both. I couldn't stop it."

I thought I'd done well, making it through the story thus far—past what I'd thought were the worst parts—without giving into the wracking grief. But the stricken look on Ursula's face did me in. I'd shed tears for her before, and now she wept for me, mirroring my terrible sorrow.

"I couldn't stop it," I told her again. Suddenly weak with the memory, I slid down the wall to sit on the carpeted floor. Ursula sat with me, her silver-clad legs crossed under the split gown, looking almost girlish, nothing of the regal queen or vicious warrior in her now.

She took one of my hands in hers. "No, Harlan, you couldn't have stopped it. They did it, not you. You bear no guilt for this."

I nodded so she'd feel better, though I knew the guilt was in fact all mine, and knuckled away the tears. "Fortunately, they didn't whip Inga and Helva much." I barked out a laugh, bitter. "*Much.* How's that for temporizing?"

"It's meaningful," Ursula insisted. "Your sisters were young, naïve, tender—it would've been easy to make them cry without hurting them severely, especially if the goal was to goad you."

"I'm not sure that helps."

"Set it aside for now, but you might find it does help, over time."

"When did you get so smart?" I touched her cheek and she smiled at me, watery.

"From being around you, obviously." She cocked her head. "Why didn't you lie, give them some story for where she'd gone?"

"Two reasons: first, because I didn't know. I was afraid of inadvertently putting them on her trail. Second, I knew it wouldn't end anything. When they didn't find her, they'd just come back to me, and do it all again, only escalating faster. The Konyngrrs don't give up easily." I gave her a humorless smile. "I come by my stubbornness honestly."

"So you had to stop it. The *Skablykrr* training."

I sobered. "Exactly. I stole out of the Imperial Palace for the second time in my life—which, as you may recall from Jepp's reports, was by no means an easy task—and I spent six months with the monks of *Skablykrr*."

"And no one found you?"

"Oh, they knew where I was, all right, but even the emperor didn't dare violate the sanctity of the *Skablykrr*. And when I returned to the Imperial Palace, they left me alone."

"But you left a third time. The final time."

"Yes. I couldn't live there. Couldn't be part of any of that any longer. I stayed a few months, recruited some friends, and we stole away. Had some adventures." I grinned, crookedly, and she smiled back. "I traveled the world, looking for my sister. Eventually I formed the Vervaldr, taking any job in a place I hadn't yet searched. Later I ended up here, thinking I might find her somewhere in these lands. Instead, hlyti has guided my footsteps to you."

"And your family just let you go?"

"Oh, they'd stripped me of my rank and disinherited me already. And they knew they'd get nothing out of me since the vows I'd taken couldn't be broken."

"*Couldn't?*" she repeated with emphasis.

I cupped her hands in mine, looking into her gray eyes, so keen and troubled. "*Can't.* It's nearly a magical binding—could be magical, for all I know—but the information I consigned to secrecy is beyond my ability to speak. I literally cannot say my eldest sister's name, or certain details I omitted. Even telling you all of this has been … painful in a way I can't quite describe."

"Thank you," she said gravely, gripping my hands. "I apologize that I ever doubted you."

"You had good reason," I said gravely. "I'm sorry for it."

She shook her head. "No, I don't think I did have good reason. But I can promise I'll never doubt you again."

I frowned a little. "Don't be hasty in—"

"I swear," she interrupted me viciously, "that I will never doubt you again, as long as I live. In the name of the boy you were and the girl she was, and the man you've made yourself into, and the woman she is, out there somewhere, I so swear."

My heart, so raw and bleeding, felt as if it swelled in my chest. "I love you, Ursula, with everything in me. The *Elskastholrr* is a vow like the others, something that cannot be broken, but even if it could be, I'll always love you. You are the best part of me. You can send me away from you, but know that it would end me. Nothing they could do to me could break me, but losing you from my life surely would."

She let go of our joined hands to crawl back onto my lap, straddling my outstretched legs and framing my face in her hands. The summer sun set her hair on fire and her eyes shone as clear and bright as Danu's sword. "I will never send you away, Harlan. You might wish to go, but it would break me to lose you, too."

"I'll never leave you willingly," I breathed, her lips coming tantalizingly close.

"Don't make that promise just yet," she urged, "but would you make me forget, for a while? I want to be only us, if only for another hour."

I didn't ask what she meant, for I knew we had yet to get to the second issue she'd closeted us to discuss. Instead I did as my queen commanded, taking her fierce mouth with mine, savoring her heat and flavor, relishing how she surrendered to my touch. My Essla, who melted only for me. Her lips parted, bringing me in, her hands working to unlace my shirt, caressing my chest. She'd long ago discovered how her calluses aroused me and she used them to good effect, with urgency and skill.

I groaned, loosing the chains I'd kept on the desire evoked by the healing, the need flooding me. For her and only her. My warrior queen. With a growl, I tumbled her onto her back, catching her wrists and pinning them. She glared at me in defiance. "Do your worst," she hissed, using her lithe strength to attempt to squirm out of my grip. Not quite shapeshifting, but slithery and as difficult to contain.

I bared my teeth at her. "You awakened the dragon, little hawk, and I plan to eat you alive."

~ 11 ~

S HE FOUGHT ME. Never an easy conquest, my warrior queen, but I had ahold of her and wouldn't let her go. The struggle roused us both to panting, the fire burning hot between us. I'd first seduced her by enticing her into a fight, earning first her respect, then her heated surrender.

It had been the end of a long and subtle siege. A brilliant stroke of strategy on my part, one I had no qualms in congratulating myself on, figuring out I'd have to batter down those walls she'd built so long ago to keep anyone from hurting her again. Sometimes she came to me easily, with the soft kisses and sweet yielding of long familiarity.

Other times she insisted I fight my way through, proving to us both the intensity of our need—mine to have her, and hers to admit me to the inner circle of her trust.

With teeth and hands, I tore away her clothing and her reserve, driving her wild as I did, until I had her naked, all long-limbed, lean woman. My Essla doesn't think she's beautiful, but only because she can't see herself as I do. Her long, elegant legs, her slim, rangy body, very nearly delicate, if not for the wiry muscles and the scars of many battles, like a tiger's stripes, evidence of her ferocity. Pinning her, I took the prominent nipple of one of her small breasts into my mouth, locking it against my palate with my tongue and allowing my upper teeth to scrape her tender flesh.

She threw back her head, swanlike throat exposed, and arched her spine, crying out in her pleasure. The sound might carry through the open windows, but we'd both passed the point of caring. I slid down her body, tracing the lines of her rib cage, the narrow waist I could span with my hands, and lingering over the quivering muscles of her abdomen, still too hollow.

The scars there had faded extensively with the magical healing, but remained pinker than the older ones. Obviously not the work of a blade, the scars knotted like an exotic blossom, petals curling from where the High Priestess of Deyrr's clawed fingers had plunged through Ursula's flesh like melted butter.

"Harlan," Ursula said, her fingers stroking through my short hair, all soothing and sweetness, battle fire forgotten. "I'm alive. I'm fine. They're scars only."

I looked up her long body, to where she'd raised herself up on one elbow to look at me when I'd paused so long. She regarded me with concern.

"I know," I told her. "I tell myself that. All the time."

She sat up, drawing me with her, stroking her hands over my chest and shoulders. Not to arouse this time, but in comfort. "I understand better now what it meant to you to be held helpless by the High Priestess's magic, not to be able to act to protect me."

My breath caught hard and agonizing in my chest, my heart straining with it.

"But it wasn't your fault," she insisted, remorseless and intent, ducking her head to catch my gaze and hold it.

I shook my head slowly. "It feels like it was."

"I get that, but it's not real."

"I swore to protect you when I swore the *Elskastholrr*. I swore to myself that I'd never stand by and fail to act when someone was being wrongfully hurt." The cries and broken weeping of my sisters echoed in my mind. They hadn't begged—nor had they ever looked at me—but they had eventually wept. The whipping master knew his job too well.

Ursula's mouth, hot and avid on mine, broke through the agonizing reverie. "None of us is invincible," she murmured against my lips. "All we can do is our best. And your best, my mighty one, is astonishing. We've made it through fights no one should have lived through." She pushed me onto my back, divesting me of my clothes and following with mouth and hands, conquering me. Making me forget. "We did it by fighting together. You at my back and me at yours."

Her hands found my rigid cock, gripping firmly, teasing in their feminine roughness. I caught my breath again, but in shock at the sheer rush of pleasure, my heart hammering now with lust. She straddled me, glorious in the pour of afternoon sunlight, Danu's chosen, and lowered herself slowly onto my cock, eyes erotically silver. So fierce and beautiful. Mine. I gave myself over to it, the sense of coming home, of her slick heat enclosing me, internal muscles clasping me.

"I don't care about your vows," she said, fully seated on me, unmoving. "Any of them. It's not your job to protect me. We protect each other. Take care of each other. Don't leave me."

"I never have. Never will," I promised, my brain fogging, my control fraying. "What else do I have to promise for you to move already?"

She laughed, delighted, throwing her head back in utter ease. So far she'd come from the rigid and scarred woman she'd been, so afraid to touch and be touched. People did heal. They did survive to live. To live good lives, despite everything.

Ursula rocked herself on me, a mischievous smile quirking her lips. Playful and pleased with herself. "You feel so good inside me, maybe I'll just stay here." She leaned to run her hands over my chest and shoulders. "Keep you here like this forever, for me to feast on."

I'd let her, too. There was nothing I wouldn't give her. "I love you, my hawk."

"And I love you. I'm grateful every day that you found me, that your hlyti guided you to me." Undulating her hips, her smile turned sensual, her internal muscles rippling along my shaft to shattering effect.

"*Luta!*" I growled, all control lost. Grasping her hips, I held her as I thrust up into her. Startled, she dug her fingers into my forearms as she convulsed, clinging to me for balance, as an anchor. I thrust again and she cried out, a soft mewl of helpless pleasure she never made at any other time. A sign that she'd dropped the last of her walls and admitted me to the most private, vulnerable part of herself.

Shifting to cup her head and brace my weight, I rolled her onto her back, savoring the way she wound her long legs around me, capturing me in place even as she gave over the rhythm to me. Languid with her surrender, she draped her arms around my neck, eyes half closed as she savored the slide of our bodies. She'd often told me she loved the press of my weight on her, the solidity of full skin-on-skin, so I gave her that—finding that sweet balance of being heavy without crushing her.

Watching her face, I adjusted the depth and drive, finding the ones that would unwind her, taking her apart bit by bit. Her nails bit into me as she climbed higher, legs grappling me, her body vibrating with tension. Silvery eyes glinting through lowered lashes, her face softened in need and love. If I ever doubted, I'd only have to watch her in these unguarded moments to see her heart and what it held for me.

My own climax gathering, I counted dynasties, an old habit

to stall orgasm, accelerating my pace. She arched, convulsed, clinging to me as if she'd fall, crying out my name. Giving over, I followed her, driving myself into her sweet sheath, emptying everything I'd ever been, ever loved and suffered.

Giving it all to her.

Elskastholrr.

"AND HERE I'D intended to distract *you*," she said throatily, some time later.

I'd rolled onto my back again, as post-coital crushing is far less erotic, draping her over me. She lay in boneless abandon, her head nestled in the hollow of my shoulder, her favored spot. I traced the lines of her body, savoring this rare moment when she was utterly relaxed and without care.

If I could have her that way all the time, I would. But then she wouldn't be the woman I'd fallen in love with—a kindred spirit. Both of us shouldered the burdens of caring for those we loved, of fighting for the just cause, preventing the power-mad from consuming everything in their unfeeling greed.

"You're right," I said quietly. "We protect each other. You are no soft and sheltered maiden. I've known that all along. I fell in love with you the first time I laid eyes on you because of that."

She propped her chin on my chest, looking up at me. "Not because I reminded you of her, of what your eldest sister suffered—not even a little?"

I combed my fingers through the silky fringe of her fiery hair, admiring the sharp mind beneath. "I didn't know that about you when I first met you," I pointed out.

"You knew." She regarded me solemnly. "You've always been able to see through me."

Not always. It would be an excellent skill to have, however. "I think you would've liked each other, you and my sister."

"I look forward to meeting her someday."

"I think I have to face that she's gone forever. That it won't happen." When Ursula opened her mouth, I headed off the argument. "But you would've liked each other. Though you're very different, you share the same sweetness, the same purity of a truly good heart."

"I'm not sweet, Harlan," she said, and her voice held a hint of hardness, the first of her defenses going into place again.

She started to move and I held her there. Not fighting my grip, she subsided easily, her expression holding a question. "Don't go yet," I said, not sure what else I could say. *Don't say the words that will end this forever.*

"I'm not." She glanced out the window. "But we have formal dinner this evening, with our guests—including your brother, unless you've changed your mind about killing him?" She raised her brows at the question, humor in her eyes.

I laughed, loving her all the more, impossible as that seemed. "No." With a sigh, I released her and sat up. The idyll couldn't last. "I lost my head this morning. It won't happen again."

"I think you get a pass on that one," she replied, strolling naked to the washbasin, her tightly muscled buttocks flexing with her warrior's stride, the subtle flare of her hips swaying slightly. She tossed me a wet cloth, and I caught it as I stood, using it to clean myself and watching her dress again in the outfit she'd had on before.

Not a good sign, that. She'd have to change to a more elaborate gown for formal dinner, but she'd chosen her court garb instead of a lounging robe for the interim, which meant she wanted to feel armored for this battle with me. Salena's rubies glinted with a fiery gleam at her ears and on a bracelet she donned again, taking comfort in her mother's jewels.

With a mental sigh for it, I donned my own clothes, including my boots, since she had. "All right, then," I said, sitting again at the table and serving us both with more food. We'd barely eaten before. Knowing Ursula, she'd be too busy watching the political currents and guiding discussion to eat much at dinner. "Out with it. What is this terrible news?"

~ **12** ~

"I MENTIONED THIS morning that I've been receiving messages from Dasnaria," she began in a neutral tone, gaze on her food, not me.

"That you believe might be from Inga. You didn't say why, other than that they sound feminine in tone."

She flicked me a glance, both of us recalling that conversation and how it had ended. "Jepp said that Inga indicated she would remain in communication if she could."

I sat back, surprised. Jepp hadn't told me that, though she'd relayed greetings and good wishes from Inga and Helva both. "Is there a reason you didn't tell me that?" I inquired, as evenly as possible.

"Yes," she replied in the same tone, "because I paid less attention to it than I should have. It didn't occur to either Jepp or me that Inga meant she'd send coded information on the politics inside the Imperial Palace. I underestimated her."

I nodded, accepting that. Inga had changed a great deal then, from the girl I'd known, if she'd indeed decided to betray the empire and had worked out a way to do it. "How is she getting messages out?"

"An excellent question and one I don't have the answer to. The messages arrive with other ones from within the Thirteen, marked as personal correspondence, written in Common

Tongue, and apparently full of gossip from a cousin by marriage."

"You don't have any cousins who aren't Tala," I mused.

"Exactly. So she knows enough about me to include that information to tip me off. She also regularly speaks of my consort's continuing good health, she and her sister sending him love and the best of wishes."

I closed my eyes briefly, the surge of old affection taking me unawares. Until that moment I hadn't realized how much I missed them. Perhaps coming to terms with losing Jenna, letting her go after all this time, allowed me to remember the good parts of our lives, and how I'd loved my other sisters, too.

"She also warns me that my consort might face some sort of competition," Ursula continued, her tone exceedingly neutral. "With the code she's using, it hasn't been clear to me what she meant—a threat against you or something else. That's another reason I haven't mentioned it to you." Her eyes were clear and without guile when I looked at her.

I continued to play this her way. "What sorts of competition does she describe?"

Ursula gave an irritated shrug. "It's couched in silly phrases; you likely to lose a tournament—when we know you don't participate in such things—or being disqualified from some sort of gaming championship. Nonsense."

I grunted noncommittally, beginning to form an idea of what might be coming.

"Now Kral has received a formal communication, delivered to the *Hákyrling*, from your brother, Emperor Hestar."

Glad I'd had the wit not to be caught with food to choke on or wine to spit, I shoved my plate away and leaned my elbows on the table, cupping a fist in my hand and propping my chin on them. That way I'd be less likely to strangle her. "It's taken you *this* long to mention that?"

Her eyes snapped sword-sharp with irritation. "If you'd controlled your temper—words I *never* thought I'd have to say to you—you would've been there to hear the news at the same time I did. Then you had to dash yourself brainless against a shapeshifter and we had a lot of old secrets to clear off the table, which was also your doing. Don't second-guess me in this, Harlan."

I took a breath and let it go. "Fine. What does this communication from my esteemed brother offer?" I knew what it would be, from Inga's hints, in my bones—from knowing my family so well, perhaps—and only needed to hear the words.

"It contains an offer of alliance. A marriage of state, between me and your brother Ban."

And there it was. It almost didn't hurt, I'd been braced for that particular blow for so long. "Don't accept Ban," I told her. "He's never been right in the head. Hold out for Mykal, or one of the twins."

She gaped at me. I didn't often catch Ursula flat-footed. Sadly I couldn't enjoy it this time. Determinedly I bit into a leg of meat, chewing, counting the beats of silence until the explosion.

"That's your response." She was entirely astonished—and quiet with it. I would've preferred the explosion.

"Yes—the best advice I can give. Ban was born wrong. He's fine in body, but not all there in his mind. Though that might be useful for your purposes." As soon as the words escaped my mouth, I regretted them. So much for keeping my cool.

"I don't deserve that," she said quietly.

"No." I blew out a breath. "I apologize. Though offering you Ban *is* an insult. Mykal or one of the twins would be more fitting for you to marry."

"Harlan. I'm not marrying any of them."

"What did Hestar offer?"

"What?"

I wiped the grease from my hands, giving her a knowing look. "A marriage of alliance with Dasnaria gets what for the High Throne of the Thirteen Kingdoms?" I phrased it deliberately, if unfairly prodding her, emphasizing where we both knew her responsibilities lay.

"Independent ally of the empire," she replied, eyeing me. "One hundred years of that status, with options to renegotiate. Protection from the Temple of Deyrr."

"A good offer," I acknowledged. "Better than I expected."

"If Hestar doesn't renege."

"He won't. Not on the letter of the agreement. Konyngrrs revere a good contract." I smiled at her in reminder of the Vervaldr's initial contract, how Ursula had pored over it, looking for loopholes, and how she hadn't believed at first that I'd written it. But she didn't smile at the old joke.

"And Deyrr?" she asked pointedly.

I lifted a shoulder and let it fall, contemplating. If I focused on the politics, I could set emotion aside. Giving Ursula advice was part of supporting her as I'd sworn to do. "I imagine Hestar will be very careful of exactly what he promises regarding Deyrr. From what we know of the movements of the High Priestess and the previous actions of the temple, I doubt Hestar has as much control there as he'd like. It's entirely possible this offer is a sign that he recognizes he needs this alliance—and your assistance—to tear Deyrr from his own throat."

"What possible assistance can I offer the Empire of Dasnaria?"

"You rule Annfwn," I pointed out. "The Tala are the descendants of n'Andana, ancient enemy of Deyrr. Arguably a successful enemy, as they made the deciding move in their long war by taking magic out of circulation and starving Deyrr of magic. In Hestar's place, who else would you bet on to contain Deyrr other than the people who did it before?"

She had an arrested look on her face, thinking through the ramifications, then wrinkled her nose. "Logical, except I don't actually rule Annfwn. Even Andi and Rayfe are hard-pressed to govern that lot of anarchists and iconoclasts."

Though I appreciated her attempt at levity, I didn't take the distraction. "Hestar doesn't know that. Something has pushed him to this point and it's an opportunity you can't afford to pass up."

Fury crossed her face like a summer squall, quickly passing. "How can you suggest that so calmly?"

I only wished I felt calm inside, but I could present the façade to ease this for her. Sliding a fruit tart onto her plate, I bit into one of my own. Fresh strawberries, first of the season, and a fair amount of sour with the sweet. "We always knew this day would come," I said after swallowing, since she'd left the question out there for me to answer, staring me down. "You've known all your life that part of being heir to the High Throne meant making a marriage of state."

"That changed for me when I committed to being with you," she replied, an edge to her voice. "I've told you that countless times."

"Essla." I set down the tart and took her hand. It lay limp and cold in mine, nothing there for me to grasp. "The *Elskastholrr* is about me and my own internal compass. Nothing changed for you. Your loyalty has always been to the High Throne first, as it has to be. You said as much this morning."

"I was angry."

"Yes, but you also know it's true."

"I don't know that."

"Oh, will you abdicate then? Step down and hand over responsibility for your Thirteen Kingdoms to… well, let's see." I pretended to think, letting go of her hand to cross my arms and rub my chin thoughtfully. "Andi is next in line, but she's preoccupied with defending Annfwn and we need her there as she's our best sorceress. Never mind the political unrest it would cause, putting a shapeshifting sorceress on the High Throne. Then there's Ami, who's come a long way but would be the first to tell everyone she's not equipped to be High Queen—and who you noted won't be pried out of her cozy nest in Windroven. Astar is your official heir, of course, but I'm not sure a toddler on the throne during a time of war is a good—"

"Just stop it," she cut me off, scowling. "Do you always have to be so thriced logical about every Danu-cursed thing?"

"Yes." I took up my strawberry tart again, savoring the sweet that came with the sour. "I do, because you're the passionate one in this relationship. You are the fiery blade while I'm the cool water of reason."

She narrowed her eyes at me. "Says he who declared I'd unleashed the dragon and promised to eat me alive."

I waved that away. "That was sex."

"And who came close to killing his brother this morning."

"A temporary lapse."

"Who was passionate enough to save his sister and gave up everything to start a new and better life."

"She gave up *her* life," I answered. "She gave up *everything*. How could I do less?"

Ursula sat back, weary, grief in her eyes. "Harlan—how can you want me to marry another man, your own brother?"

"All I want is to do my best by you, and you need to do your best by your realm. That means accepting this alliance. You'd be marrying into the imperial family of the Dasnarian Empire, gaining a century of reprieve and very likely averting a war. That is a service to the High Throne that will save countless lives and bloodshed. There really isn't a question here of what you should do."

"I could marry you," she pointed out. "You're full brother to the emperor."

"No, I'm not. I was disinherited, stripped of rank. In the eyes of my family, I no longer exist."

"If I'm married to you, and they want this alliance, they might reconsider that."

Unfamiliar bitterness rose along with my gorge and I regretted drinking so much wine earlier. "I wouldn't have them," I bit out.

"Not even for me?" she asked, cagey now, neatly boxing me in. "You say you'll do whatever I need, but you won't take back a title that matters nothing to you? Won't take the opportunity for them to restore what's rightfully yours, something they should never have taken from you, particularly since you acted only in the best interests of another member of the family?" Ursula tipped her head in thought. "I wonder what Jenna would say you should do?"

I stared at her, astounded. Flummoxed. She'd outmaneuvered me again and I'd never seen it coming. If only I could go back to bed and magically start this entire day anew. "This is why you wanted the story about my eldest sister before you told me about the marriage offer."

She smiled thinly. "You're not the only one who's learned a few things about managing an obstinate spouse."

"I am not your spouse, hawk," I ground out.

"Oh, rabbit, you most surely are. All that's lacking is the actual contract and I happen to know you've a deft hand with those." She raised her brows as she scored the point, letting me know she hadn't missed my earlier reference to that.

"A missing contract creates a rather large hole."

"Easily fixed. You're going to marry me, Harlan, tonight. Your brother will stand witness for you and Zynda for me. Then Kral can deliver the news to Hestar that I'm fortuitously already married to a Prince of Dasnaria, and we can hammer out an agreement of alliance."

I had no words. "Ursula. I—"

I don't know what I would've said, because the lookout's alarm shout and the pealing of the warning bells—straight to second-level alarm—dashed everything else from my mind.

~ 13 ~

BOTH ON OUR feet in the same movement, we grabbed the weapons we always kept at hand as we dashed through her rooms and into the hall. Side by side, we ran through the arcade and her private courtyard, taking the shortcut to the walls, her innate speed making up for my longer stride.

A roaring shadow passed over us, an inferno of flame heating the summer air to crackling. Zynda in dragon form, blazing a swath through the summer sky at an enemy I couldn't see without stopping to scrutinize. Glad she was on top of our defense, and that I could recognize her now, I made a mental note to establish a system for us to warn of friendly dragon approach. It didn't bear thinking what a dragon bent on destroying us could do.

Shouts over the cacophony of the alarm bells greeted us in the outer yard as Ursula's protective guard formed around her. Other fighters streamed in from various quarters, some still buckling on weapons. "To the walls," she commanded crisply.

I turned to her. "You know you should go to—"

She rounded on me with a vicious glare. "Don't do this now. I'm done with being protected. This is *my* castle, *my* realm, and I'm done cowering indoors while you all fight for me."

I reassessed, taken aback by her vehemence, then nodded and tapped the flat of my broadsword to my forehead.

"*Elskastholrr*," I told her, and she grinned, a feral baring of teeth.

"Damn straight."

"Your Majesty!" The current gate commander dashed over. "Permission to close the gates?"

We exchanged a glance. The alarm bells had been ringing only a minute or so. "Do we have people outside still making for the castle?" she asked.

"Yes, but—"

"Gates stay up until they're all in," she ordered, turning her back and running for the walls.

We climbed the ladders swiftly, taking in the scene. I couldn't make much sense of what I saw at first. Smoke rose from the fields and orchards, thick and unnaturally coiling, dimming the air and swarming over people on the road—running either for the safety of town or the castle walls—or over people lying immobile. Zynda the dragon turned on wingtip—which seemed to bring her dangerously close to the ground—her silhouette against the afternoon sun very nearly vertical in the sky, Marskal clearly outlined on her back.

Brant ran up to us, out of breath. "Captain!" For a moment I didn't know if he meant me or if he'd reverted to the Hawks' habit of calling Ursula "captain." In the heat of the fight, it didn't matter. "Attack by unknown entities."

"Be more specific," Ursula snapped, eyes on the scene, also scanning.

Was the smoke…feeding on the people who were down? Clouds of it coalesced around their fallen forms, while other masses seemed more condensed, taking shape. They seemed almost humanoid, except terribly distorted, with missing limbs in places, appendages in others that looked more animal. Or like nothing natural at all.

"Can't." Brant replied. "Looks like smoke, but with particles like ash. Drops people where they stand. We can't pinpoint the source and—"

I swore, viciously, and they both turned to me in expectation. "Ash," I spat out. "Curse us for worse than fools. Those places are where we scattered the ashes of the unidentified dead."

When they stared blankly, I clarified. "After Illyria's defeat, all of the people she converted with her Deyrr magic—we burned them when the pieces kept coming."

"I remember that," Ursula said. Brant nodded, though he hadn't been one of the Hawks then. It had been terrible, soul-crushing duty and my Vervaldr, with the great gift of not recognizing most of the victims as friends and family, had handled the bulk of it.

"Some victims were identified and their ashes taken home to family graveyards." I waved my broadsword at the unusually fertile fields and orchards this summer. "The rest we spread on the tilled earth, as is traditional in Dasnaria. Stupid and short-sighted."

Ursula spun to survey the area. Zynda dove and flew so low she could only glide, as a downstroke of her wings would hit ground. "You're saying that smoke is the undead ash, rising again?"

"The remains are still coming," I replied grimly. "Even as ash. Unforgivably stupid of me to keep it so near the castle."

"My people would have done the same," she replied absently, attention keen on the people fleeing the attacking smoke. Assisted by squads of Ordnung troops, some of the people on the road had unharnessed their horses from the laden wagons, riding full speed for the castle gates. A group of young women in pretty gowns ran, ribbons streaming. One lost her hat and it flew to the road behind her. She started to turn, but a soldier passing her on horseback shouted and pointed at the gates, then charged a cloud of smoke that had descended on the hat. "Ashes to earth, the cycle of life," Ursula added.

"Only this ash has nothing of life in it," I observed.

"What of the people down—what does the smoke do?"

"Near as we can tell it suffocates them," Brant answered. "Before they drop, it seems like they can't breathe."

"Does anything stop it?" she asked, her gaze on her fallen people. The soldier who'd charged the cloud of smoke was in trouble, he and the horse spinning as the smoke raked them with claws that should've been insubstantial but had them convulsing.

"Nothing so far," Brant answered. "Weapons pass through it."

Ursula dug her fingers into the parapet as she leaned over, clearly wishing to leap over it and into the fight. "All advancing on Ordnung. The walls won't keep it out."

"No, Your Majesty."

"Dragon fire might do it," I said, pointing as Zynda came around. She spouted a blast of flame through a cloud of ash where there weren't any people. We all leaned forward to watch. The ash disappeared in the flame, but in the wake of her passage, the air eddied with oily black shadows, the ash condensing again into coils, then into humanoid shape—and continued to move toward the castle.

"No good," Ursula murmured. "Why this, why today?"

"Does it matter?" Brant muttered darkly.

"It might. This is magic. You fight magic with magic. The ash has been there since last autumn. Why did it wake today?"

"It's midsummer," Kelleah said. She returned our surprised gazes with imperturbable calm. Of course she would've come to the walls, in case anyone needed her healing skills, not knowing we had nothing to fight. Would she be able to help the fallen?

We'd have to retrieve them first, risking more of us.

"Midsummer," Ursula echoed, realization in her voice.

"You call it the Feast of Danu, and Danu is your goddess, not mine," Kelleah supplied, a pointed reminder.

Ursula had discussed—and quickly dismissed—celebrating the Feast of Danu, but the holiday had fallen out of fashion with the population under Uorsin's rule. He'd promoted worship of Glorianna and Her church as the primary religion for the Twelve Kingdoms. With so much else to do and really no one to champion the event, any thoughts of celebrating Danu's Day at midsummer had faded before they'd fully formed.

"But even in Annfwn we observe the longest day of the year," Kelleah noted. "As it's a day full of the potent magic of life."

"Enough to raise the undead," Ursula murmured, eyes still on the running women. Mounted soldiers had picked up two, but three others still jogged slowly, hampered by their pretty summer gowns. "The question is how do we put them to rest again?"

I measured the distance with her, and the relentless pace of the smoke creatures, many of them congealing into shape now. They'd soon reach the castle. How do you wall out something like that? Unless we could find a way to nullify it, the stuff would slowly suffocate everyone in Ordnung.

"We can't put them to rest," I realized. Ursula glanced over at my abrupt tone. "The ash has to be utterly destroyed," I told her. "Here and everywhere."

She blanched, swiftly following my meaning, then turned to one of her guard who also ran messages. "Have Shua draft a proclamation, short, as many copies as possible to be distributed throughout Mohraya as quickly as possible, and then beyond. Any ashes of victims of Illyria that have been buried, scattered, sealed in crypts or urns—whatever it might be—should be avoided or kept locked away. Anyone in possession of these remains should notify Ordnung so we can deal with it."

The guard took off at a dead run and everyone looked at Ursula expectantly for the solution. She looked to me. I had nothing.

"Zynda can magic it away. I've seen it," Jepp said, arriving out of breath with Kral behind her. He met my gaze steadily, tossing me an ironic salute, gaze going to the scene below and eyes widening in incredulity.

"Call them in," Ursula ordered Brant.

He relayed the message to Dary, once again atop the watchtower, who employed her flags to signal Marskal using the Hawks' code.

"You can call them in," Kral drawled, "but your precious sorceress refuses to use the power, remember?"

"She doesn't like to *abuse* the power." Jepp rolled her eyes at him. "Something you could stand to learn, Your Imperial Highness."

He narrowed his eyes at her, then lifted a shoulder and let it fall, laughing. "Not so much of a danger anymore, as I no longer possess that title. All your fault, hystrix."

"You too?" I asked, somewhat surprised—mostly at how little my brother, who'd once held ambition above all else, seemed to care.

"As our esteemed elder brother recently took pains to remind me," Kral replied, gaze icing as he met mine. For a moment we shared a strange camaraderie, both exiled princes, stripped of our titles. And both strangely in this place.

Wind from Zynda's wings buffeted us, and we all reflexively crouched. Marskal slid down the dragon's extended leg, landing neatly beside us on the wall. He used a network of ropes that made a sort of harness on her great body.

"Nicely done," I told him.

He nodded in appreciation. "We've been working out the system. Hoping to use similar harnesses with other winged shapeshifter and human-form fighting pairs in battle."

The dragon became a hummingbird in midair—an astonishing collapse of size—who then zoomed in to hover beside Marskal before transforming into Zynda.

"I notice you didn't try *that* form against me," I noted.

She grinned. "Too easily eaten, even by a mossback."

"Enough banter," Ursula ordered crisply. "Zynda—Jepp thinks you can use Tala magic to destroy the ash, which we believe to be the risen remains of Illyria's undead."

Zynda's easy smile vanished as her gaze went to Jepp, contemplating the scout. "Hmm," was the only sound she made.

"Did your dragon fire work on it?" Jepp asked pointedly.

With an annoyed turn to her mouth, Zynda shook her head. "You saw it didn't, which is irritating, because dragon fire works on *everything*. The ash does avoid my magic-nullifying presence though—we noted that much."

"But goes right back when you've passed," Ursula said.

Zynda acknowledged that glumly.

"Zynda." Marskal took her by the shoulders, facing her with a serious expression. "You've said that you don't like to use sorcery because it takes creatures out of the cycle of life—but Illyria's undead are already unnatural. Wouldn't eliminating that ash be restoring balance?"

She frowned at him, searching his face. "A neat argument," she finally replied, "and I'm not sure your logic is entirely correct, but you all seem agreed there's no other way to stop this stuff?"

"No," I answered, taking charge as Captain of Ordnung's

defense. "And it's coming this way. It doesn't matter if we close the gates, the walls won't keep it out. If you won't do this, Zynda, then we need to come up with other options fast or everyone here will die."

"I'd be happier with an enemy I could cleave with my sword," Kral growled.

"Or take apart with daggers," Jepp added.

Ursula threw them both an appreciative look. Something settled inside me, a realignment of sorts, that we were all the same side. Hlyti had guided my footsteps to this time and place—and these people—but so too had it brought Kral. Two points of the triangle, bound together.

With a third still out there. For the first time in years and years, I entertained hope that Jenna might also find her way here. If we survived this.

"I'll do it," Zynda decided. "Though I'm unprepared, so it will take a bit to build the necessary power to clear an area this big."

She became a hummingbird again. Jewel bright, she zoomed to the watchtower, where hopefully Dary wouldn't be too startled.

Ursula shaded her eyes, staring up at the tower that now held two women. "She didn't wait for instructions," she complained.

"She knows what to do," Marskal murmured beside her, mirroring her stance. "Your Majesty," he added belatedly, then grinned at whatever Ursula muttered under her breath at him.

"She's used a lot of magic today already," Ursula noted, a hint of worry in it, "lots of shapeshifting and healing." She deliberately didn't look at me. "I hope she's up to this."

"She is," Marskal replied definitely. "Dragon form has launched her into a new level of ability—beyond what any of us might have predicted."

"Is that so?" Ursula looked over to me at last, raising her brows. "Finally, some good news."

I smiled back at her.

She and Marskal fell into conversation, discussing countermeasures should Zynda's effort fail. He summoned several Hawks and they sent them running with messages to secure people in parts of the castle without outside egress.

I scanned the strange battlefield, the fallen on the ground, the prowling smoke creatures. Groups of guards herded people toward town, giving rides to stragglers. A cadre of messengers on fast horses burst from the castle, moving too fast for the smoke monsters to catch them, the dust of their wake quickly settling, unlike the unnatural ash. We could take Ursula out of the castle the same way. I glanced at her, taking in her wide stance on the walls of Ordnung, in her element as she made fast decisions and crisply issued orders.

I'd never pry her out of her castle either.

The only people left on the road were the three young women, who were clearly winded but still struggling up the incline to the castle gates. A cloud of clawed creatures emerged from a copse of trees, advancing on them from the side. All the other troops were engaged elsewhere, leaving them unprotected.

Measuring their relative speeds—the exhausted young ladies in their fancy slippers not meant for such rigor, and the billowing humanoid ash figures—I knew the women would never make it.

I couldn't stand by and do nothing. With Ursula focused on protecting Ordnung, I stepped back, then shimmied down the nearest ladder and ran.

With any luck, I'd be back before she noticed I'd left.

~ 14 ~

I BOLTED THROUGH the gates, with a snapping gesture recruiting two more gate guards to accompany me. They obeyed with practiced alacrity. With the incline in our favor, we raced for the young women. Their faces red with exertion, they cried out when they saw us, holding out their arms in stark fear.

Younger than I'd thought. No more than girls, perhaps in their first pretty grown-up dresses, thinking they'd have nothing more than a sweet summer afternoon outing. That's what they should've had. Nothing more than seeing the market and flirting in their summer frocks. Not this vile attack.

The two guards with me each seized a gratefully squealing girl, swinging her into their arms and running for the castle. The third girl, in a white dress with pink rosebuds, lagged behind. As I ran toward her, I saw she'd lost her slippers—or they'd fallen off in pieces, because she'd run her feet raw, blood and dust caking her feet.

The smoke creatures reached her as I did, the oily ash cloud snaking around her, the distorted faces snarling silently. She screamed, a piercing sound of agony and despair. Reaching into the cloud, I tried to yank her free of it by seizing her wrist, the resistance as strong as if actual men held her. She cried piteously as I wrenched her shoulder.

Thrice curse it. Because I had to try, I swung my broadsword over her head through the murky figures. It passed through them as if I sliced at nothing, the unimpeded swing nearly taking me off balance. Recovering, with no time to sheathe my sword as the girl now hung limp in the cluster of shadow shapes, I tossed it aside and reached in for her.

The smoked slimed over my skin, the ash like grit in my eyes and nose. Memories and emotions not my own filled my mind—violence, despair, and a grinding need to reach Ordnung, to devour the living. My lungs strained for air, my heart booming in my chest, struggling to pump blood growing thick and oily, as I wrestled the creatures for the girl.

Digging in, using all the strength I'd built over the years, fiercely glad for Kelleah's healing that had me in top form, I took one step back, then another, dragging the girl back. Some of the writhing creatures came with us, but the others dug in also. Good for me as that allowed my head at least to pop free, and I took a deep breath of clean air, like a drowning man barely able to push his face above water.

The girl had gone entirely limp, dead weight in my arms, and I struggled back with all my might.

A warrior's howl cut through the thick silence, the oily smoke parting around me as a sword cleaved it. The Deyrr creatures released their grip so abruptly that I fell back, the girl cradled in my arms.

"Give her to me," a woman in silver armor demanded.

I blinked at her in confused disbelief. Kaedrin, warrior priestess of Danu. Her brown eyes snapped with impatience in her lean face. "Give her to me," she repeated.

I relaxed my hold, and Kaedrin snatched up the girl, taking off at a run. Kelleah waited a safe distance away, wheeling to match Kaedrin's stride, already laying hands on the girl, a green light emanating out.

Skull throbbing, heart still pounding and lungs tightly laboring for breath, I tried to stand but barely managed to sit. Until I saw Ursula.

A whirlwind of black and silver, rubies shining like beacons of fire, she spun faster than a hummingbird's wings, slicing again and again at the increasingly indistinct figures. With each pass of her sword, the vaporous shapes lost human form, reduced to swirling clouds. The ruby on her sword hilt glowed with light brighter than dragon fire—but that seemed to burn the ash away as she defended me.

I struggled to my feet, trying to call for her, no breath to do it with. Reaching for her.

Ursula.

Essla.

Danu save her.

Even as I thought it, a deep blue glow washed over me, the feel of it somehow the same as the depths of Zynda's eyes. My lungs abruptly cleared, strength returning to my limbs.

The blue wave of magic expanded, pushing out until it blended with the deep blue midsummer sky. With a palpable pop, it vanished again, leaving the fields clear. The taint of ash gone again, so only golden light of the long, light-filled evening ahead remained to fall over the growing fields and ripe orchards.

Abruptly bereft of an opponent, Ursula lurched much as I had, gracefully regaining her footing in a spin that brought her to face me, a wild expression on her face. One that crumpled into relief when I opened my arms to her.

I grunted as she launched herself at me, a lithe arrow of a woman, bracing myself to absorb the impact as she rained kisses on my face, wrapping her long legs around my waist and clinging to me with all the considerable ferocity in her.

"I could fucking kill you," she said between kisses. "What in

Danu's freezing tits were you thinking?"

"That I had to do something," I said. I stopped her with a long kiss, waiting until some of the tension dissolved in her body and she relaxed in the surety of my embrace. Then looking her in the eye, I offered a rueful smile. "I couldn't just stand there and do nothing."

"I know." The knowledge showed in her steely gaze, and she sighed heavily. "You wouldn't be you if you could."

"But what in Danu were *you* thinking?" I growled, letting my fear for her turn into righteous anger. "You had no business coming after me. The High Throne comes first!"

She met my gaze evenly. "It should. I know that in my head. But in my heart, it's not true. I'll never be able to just stand there and do nothing if you're in danger."

I laughed a little at how neatly she threw my words back in my face, my own heart squeezing at the staggering impact of her declaration.

"I wouldn't be me if I could," she added, with a quirk of a smile.

Unable to frame a reply, I kissed her long and deep. When we came up for air, I set her on her feet and surveyed the area. We both retrieved our swords.

"Why did your sword work and mine didn't?" I wondered aloud.

"Salena's rubies, I think," she replied. "The thought came into my mind, bright and clear, that the rubies would disperse the magic. I needed magic and that was the only thing I could think of."

"You think Salena infused them with some sort of defensive magic?"

"Why not? The Star certainly is magic. And our mother was very specific about those rubies being distributed among her daughters. We know Salena saw far into the future."

I took her hand and we turned toward Ordnung's white towers, climbing the hill together. People streamed past us, going to collect the fallen.

"You're going to marry me tonight, yes?" Ursula asked, though it sounded more like a demand than a question.

"It's not the best decision for the throne, for the alliance with Dasnaria," I cautioned her.

She threw me a blazing look of scorn. "Do you have any other objections, besides that?"

"No." I raised her hand and turned it over, brushing a kiss over her callused palm, delighting in the shiver that ran through her. "In this, as in all things, I am yours to command."

~ EPILOGUE ~

"YOU EVER WERE the luckiest of us," Kral commented, signing his name with a flourish. "Landing in honey, after all your protests to the contrary."

I grunted in non-reply, hoping he'd drop the subject. No such luck because Kral's grin sharpened knowingly, fully his namesake the shark, scenting blood in the water. My blood.

He leaned in, dropping his voice to a conspiratorial whisper and switching to Dasnarian. "Tell me, rabbit—you had this planned all along. All that *Elskastholrr* nonsense. It was all part of an elaborate scheme to get you to this point, wasn't it?"

"Of course." I spread my hands at the spare chapel of Danu, lavishly heaped with summer blossoms and dripping with garlands, the air sweet as honey. "I intuited decades ago that Dasnaria would go to war with an obscure coalition of kingdoms where an eight-year-old princess would end up as High Queen. I figured back then that if I studied the art of *Skablykyrr*, I could work my way into her confidence and one day manipulate her into marrying me as part of an alliance to fend off conquest."

"Exceedingly clever," Kral agreed, clapping me hard enough on the back that I had to brace myself. Then he sobered. "It might not work."

"No." I scanned the small assembly, everyone in their finery, awaiting only Ursula's arrival. Kaedrin prayed quietly at Danu's altar, ready to perform the ceremony. She hadn't explained her abrupt reappearance, except to say that Danu had guided her to us because she'd been needed. The empire required only a contract, and Kral and I had drafted one—to his infinite amusement, as it bore only superficial resemblance to a traditional Dasnarian marriage contract—but Ursula and I would be wed by a priestess of the goddess of warriors as befit us both. "It likely won't satisfy Hestar, but Ursula is determined and I cannot refuse her."

Kral lifted a shoulder and let it fall. "You wouldn't be a Konyngrr if you'd stand back and allow another to take your woman, no matter the stakes. It is, after all, a grand Dasnarian tradition to make exceptionally foolhardy political choices for the sake of love. It seems your Ursula will fit right into the family. And this will surprise Hestar, so that makes it even better."

"Will you be willing to lie and say the wedding—and this contract—predate his offer?"

Kral showed a smile full of white teeth. "Oh, baby brother, I will savor every moment of defying and lying to Hestar. That fucker."

I laughed, the amusement full-hearted, and I clapped him on the back, satisfied to see him lurch forward before he caught himself. "I'm glad you're here," I told him, surprising myself that I meant it.

"I am, too." He sounded subdued, uncharacteristically so, and met my gaze. "I want to offer apology, for what I did to you and Jenna."

My heart caught, as it always did at the sound of her name, even though it had been said aloud so many times today that it should have lost its potency. It seemed Kral and I stood together again at that inn, Jenna a white ghost between us, all of us so painfully young.

"I forgive you." As I spoke the formal words, something seemed to let go inside me. "None of us are who we were then. All joking aside, none of us could have foreseen where we'd end up. Certainly not here, like this."

"True," he mused thoughtfully. "We cannot retrace those footsteps…and yet, I wish I could make amends with Jenna. I can't give her back what was stolen, but I wish her happy and would do whatever she asked of me. I owe her that."

"Jenna?"

We both turned to see Kaedrin standing there, a quizzical look on her face. The silver-haired warrior woman looked between the two of us. "I apologize for interrupting and eavesdropping. I don't understand Dasnarian, but I heard a name I know and wondered. I knew a young woman, long ago, named Jenna. Not a common name in the Thirteen Kingdoms, but she was also Dasnarian."

This pivotal day hadn't finished with me, apparently, holding yet one more shock to turn my blood to water. I stared at the priestess, unable to summon thought. Fortunately, Kral had no such issues. "Where did you know her?"

"She trained for a while at the Temple of Danu in Ehas," Kaedrin said. "My sister priestess brought her there—Kaja, who was Jepp's mother." She gestured toward Jepp, who stood conversing with Marskal, both of them smart-looking in the formal uniform of the Hawks.

"Ehas?" I repeated, able to grasp at least that nugget of information. Surely Jenna hadn't been in Ehas all this time. And at the Temple of Danu. It didn't bear considering.

"Yes." Kaedrin returned her gaze to me, her face clear and unlined, despite her age. "It had to be, oh, more than twenty years ago, but I remember Jenna. So lovely, so determined to learn to be a warrior of Danu."

Now Kral gaped along with me. "She became a warrior of Danu?" I asked, trying to imagine it.

Kaedrin smiled, enjoying our bemusement. "Indeed. She was a dancer—I don't know if you knew that—and many dances have their roots in martial forms. Kaja taught her to use knives instead of jewels within the forms she knew and I helped fill in the holes."

At last I could move. "Kaedrin," I said, and her eyes widened at the urgency in my tone, "is she still in Ehas?"

She looked rueful, shaking her head. "No. She only stayed a short time. She was running from something, which I suspect you know, so she changed her appearance and her name."

Disappointment, a sodden and familiar weight, returned to fill the spaces lightened by hope. "No wonder I could never find her," I commented.

Kral's hand fell heavy on my shoulder, and he looked at me with shared feeling. "It was too much to hope," he said, "that we might recover her after so long."

Kaedrin watched us, a canniness in her gaze. "I know where she went," she offered.

Slowly, afraid of shattering the fragile possibility, we both turned to look at the priestess, cautious, Kral's hand still on my shoulder. Neither of us seemed able to ask the most important question.

"At least, I sent her news of Kaja's passing, and I have reason to believe she received it," Kaedrin added that last enigmatically. "Do you swear before Danu that you mean her no harm?"

I went down on one knee without a thought. To my surprise, Kral joined me in the same movement. In one voice, we swore it together.

Kaedrin smiled with a soft radiance unusual for a follower of the sharp-eyed goddess. "I think Kaja would be pleased. She always promised to continue her service as Danu's handmaiden, to help us along as she saw fit. I shall give you the information, Harlan, as a wedding gift. And her new name: Ivariel."

Ivariel. I took it in, a name I could use like a balm to heal those old wounds, so recently purged.

Kaedrin's eyes lifted to the chapel entrance. "Time to begin," she said.

I rose to my feet and turned, absorbing the final stunning blow of the day—this one a punch of glory. Ursula stood framed in the chapel doorway, a vision of bright light and surpassing loveliness.

She wore a gown I'd never seen—a spectacular work of art, made entirely of finely worked metal feathers, all in shades of bronze, copper, and gold. The high collar rose to frame her long throat, a ruff of the metallic feathers radiating out from a deep bloodred at their base that matched her hair and picked up the gleam of Salena's rubies in her necklace and at her ears. From there the gown flowed in gleaming layers, sweeping down into a long, trailing skirt. Zynda, also dressed in a coppery gown, finished arranging Ursula's train and, giving her a kiss and whispering something that made her cousin smile, slipped aside for me.

I moved forward to this stunning woman who'd somehow become mine. She wore her crown and a regal smile, though a hint of uncertainty ghosted in her gray eyes.

"No sword?" I asked.

She smiled a little. "I thought I owed you that. I can come to you without weapons and trust that I'll always be safe. Tonight I'm a woman first. With you, always the woman first."

Always she knew how to outmaneuver me, taking my breath away with a few words. "I haven't seen this gown before," I commented.

"No, you haven't, because I hid it away," she replied, almost shyly. "Just in case."

"You've always been an excellent strategist," I conceded.

"Do you like it?" She asked, hesitant with the question.

"You are more beautiful in this moment than I have ever seen you," I told her gravely. "Ursula, my Essla, will you marry me and be my wife?"

The uncertainty fled, and she smiled in truth, all woman and not the queen. "Yes. Yes, I will, if you're sure?"

"I'm sure," I told her and offered her my arm.

She didn't take it right away. "I know I pushed you into this."

I laughed, took her hand and placed it firmly on my forearm. "Oh, my little hawk, you should know by now that you can't push me into doing anything I don't want to do."

With a wry smile, she huffed out a laugh. "I do know that." She narrowed her eyes. "No wedding bracelets, though, Dasnarian."

"No one could chain you, my Hawk."

Her answering smile faded as she studied me. "Why do you look so strange? Something has upset you."

She saw through me so well. "Kaedrin knows where my sister is. Her name is Ivariel now."

Ursula's eyes widened in shock. "I sense Danu's hand in this," she murmured.

"I believe that may be so."

"We'll look for her," Ursula said. "Whatever you need."

"Thank you, love." I turned her to face Danu's altar and we walked toward it, side by side, partners in this, as in all things.

Kneeling before Danu, we bowed our heads to Her clear-eyed justice and wisdom, listening as Her priestess bound us together in law and spirit as we'd long been in our hearts.

Though we had the shortest of nights to celebrate together, I fully intended to savor every sweet moment of it.

TITLES BY JEFFE KENNEDY

OTHER FANTASY ROMANCES

A COVENANT OF THORNS

Rogue's Pawn
Rogue's Possession
Rogue's Paradise

THE TWELVE KINGDOMS

Negotiation
The Mark of the Tala
The Tears of the Rose
The Talon of the Hawk
Heart's Blood
For Crown and Kingdom

THE UNCHARTED REALMS

The Pages of the Mind
The Edge of the Blade
The Snows of Windroven
The Shift of the Tide
The Arrows of the Heart
The Dragons of Summer

THE CHRONICLES OF DASNARIA

Prisoner of the Crown
Exile of the Seas
Warrior of the World

SORCEROUS MOONS

Lonen's War
Oria's Gambit
The Tides of Bára
The Forests of Dru
Oria's Enchantment
Lonen's Reign

THE FORGOTTEN EMPIRES

The Orchid Throne

CONTEMPORARY ROMANCES

Shooting Star

MISSED CONNECTIONS

Last Dance
With a Prince
Since Last Christmas

CONTEMPORARY EROTIC ROMANCES

Exact Warm Unholy
The Devil's Doorbell

FACETS OF PASSION

Sapphire
Platinum
Ruby

Five Golden Rings

FALLING UNDER

Going Under
Under His Touch
Under Contract

EROTIC PARANORMAL

MASTER OF THE OPERA E-SERIAL

Master of the Opera, Act 1: Passionate Overture
Master of the Opera, Act 2: Ghost Aria
Master of the Opera, Act 3: Phantom Serenade
Master of the Opera, Act 4: Dark Interlude
Master of the Opera, Act 5: A Haunting Duet
Master of the Opera, Act 6: Crescendo
Master of the Opera

BLOOD CURRENCY

Blood Currency

BDSM FAIRYTALE ROMANCE

Petals and Thorns

OTHER WORKS

Birdwoman
Hopeful Monsters
Teeth, Long and Sharp

Thank you for reading!

About Jeffe Kennedy

Jeffe Kennedy is an award-winning author whose works include novels, non-fiction, poetry, and short fiction. She has been a Ucross Foundation Fellow, received the Wyoming Arts Council Fellowship for Poetry, and was awarded a Frank Nelson Doubleday Memorial Award. She serves on the Board of Directors for the Science Fiction and Fantasy Writers of America (SFWA) as a Director at Large.

Her award-winning fantasy romance trilogy *The Twelve Kingdoms* hit the shelves starting in May 2014. Book 1, *The Mark of the Tala*, received a starred Library Journal review and was nominated for the RT Book of the Year while the sequel, *The Tears of the Rose* received a Top Pick Gold and was nominated for the RT Reviewers' Choice Best Fantasy Romance of 2014. The third book, *The Talon of the Hawk*, won the RT Reviewers' Choice Best Fantasy Romance of 2015. Two more books followed in this world, beginning the spin-off series *The Uncharted Realms*. Book one in that series, *The Pages of the Mind*, has also been nominated for the RT Reviewer's Choice Best Fantasy Romance of 2016 and won RWA's 2017 RITA® Award. The second book, *The Edge of the Blade*, released December 27, 2016, and is a PRISM finalist, along with *The Pages of the Mind*. The next in the series, *The Shift of the Tide*, came out in August, 2017. A high fantasy trilogy, The Chronicles of Dasnaria, taking place in *The Twelve Kingdoms* world began releasing from Rebel Base books in 2018.

She also introduced a new fantasy romance series, *Sorcerous*

Moons, which includes *Lonen's War*, *Oria's Gambit*, *The Tides of Bàra*, and *The Forests of Dru*. She's begun releasing a new contemporary erotic romance series, *Missed Connections*, which started with *Last Dance* and continues in *With a Prince* and *Since Last Christmas*.

In 2019, St. Martins Press will release the first book, *The Orchid Throne*, in a new fantasy romance series, *The Forgotten Empires*.

Her other works include a number of fiction series: the fantasy romance novels of *A Covenant of Thorns*; the contemporary BDSM novellas of the *Facets of Passion*; an erotic contemporary serial novel, *Master of the Opera*; and the erotic romance trilogy, *Falling Under*, which includes *Going Under*, *Under His Touch* and *Under Contract*.

She lives in Santa Fe, New Mexico, with two Maine coon cats, plentiful free-range lizards and a very handsome Doctor of Oriental Medicine.

Jeffe can be found online at her website: JeffeKennedy.com, every Sunday at the popular SFF Seven blog, on Facebook, on Goodreads and pretty much constantly on Twitter @jeffekennedy. She is represented by Sarah Younger of Nancy Yost Literary Agency.

jeffekennedy.com

facebook.com/Author.Jeffe.Kennedy

twitter.com/jeffekennedy

goodreads.com/author/show/1014374.Jeffe_Kennedy

Sign up for her newsletter here.

jeffekennedy.com/sign-up-for-my-newsletter

www.ingramcontent.com/pod-product-compliance
Lightning Source LLC
Chambersburg PA
CBHW032037180726
48284CB00008B/2632